Gargantua

Gargantua

The most horrific life of the great Gargantua
father of Pantagruel

Composed once upon a time by M. Alcofribas,
the abstractor of the quintessence.
A book full of Pantagruelism.
Available in Lyons,
at François Juste's bookshop,
near Our Lady of Comfort.

François Rabelais

Translated by Andrew Brown

ET REMOTISSIMA PROPE

100 PAGES

100 PAGES

Published by Hesperus Press Limited
4 Rickett Street, London SW6 1RU
www.hesperuspress.com

Gargantua first published in French in 1534
This translation first published by Hesperus Press Limited, 2003

Introduction and English language translation © Andrew Brown, 2003
Foreword © Paul Bailey, 2003

Designed and typeset by Fraser Muggeridge
Printed in the United Arab Emirates by Oriental Press

ISBN: 1-84391-057-8

CONTENTS

Foreword by Paul Bailey　　　　　　　　　　　　vii
Introduction　　　　　　　　　　　　　　　　　　xi

Gargantua　　　　　　　　　　　　　　　　　　　1
　Notes　　　　　　　　　　　　　　　　　　　143

Biographical note　　　　　　　　　　　　　151

'Writing should laugh, not weep,' writes François Rabelais at the end of his dedicatory poem to the Reader, and adds, 'Since laughter is of man the very marrow.' This sentiment, and his unique expression of it, have kept his anarchic art alive for going on five centuries. Along with his near-contemporaries Cervantes and Shakespeare, comparatively little is known about his life, though diligent scholars have been unearthing curious facts about him since his death in 1553. According to the *Oxford English Dictionary*, the word 'Rabelaisian' entered the language as late as 1817, and it hasn't gone away. Everyone who uses it knows that it implies a certain coarseness, even lewdness, and that it suggests physical extravagance. The word can be employed to register either admiration or disgust, depending on the moral or religious convictions of the speaker. This writer who, more than any other, is forever associated with the basic functions of the human body, was born and raised a Roman Catholic and did not abandon the faith.

I remember, when I first read James Joyce's *Ulysses* in my early twenties, how startled I was when Leopold Bloom 'kicked open the crazy door of the jakes', undid his braces, lowered his trousers carefully and sat himself down to read the morning paper: '…he allowed his bowels to ease themselves gently as he read, reading still patiently, that slight constipation of yesterday quite gone.' People went to the lavatory in the real world, but not in *books*, I thought, crassly. It was this luminously truthful scene, combined with Molly Bloom's soliloquy, that so offended Virginia Woolf, the arid High Priestess of literary decorum. The respected French critic and translator Valéry Larbaud expressed a different view. In a letter to Joyce's friend and patron Sylvia Beach, he wrote, 'I am raving mad over *Ulysses*. The book is as great and comprehensive and human as Rabelais.'

We know that Rabelais was acquainted with many of the noted humanists of the sixteenth century, and that he corresponded with Erasmus, the most illustrious of them all. He studied medicine and was cognisant of the principal ailments of the age, especially the pox, which swept across Europe in the 1400s. The genital disease, given the name 'syphilis' in 1530 by the Italian physician and poet Girolamo Fracastoro in his poem *Syphilis, sive Morbus Gallicus*, is a constant in the writings of Rabelais. It's there as a term of contempt or irritation, but also as an enemy of the body and mind. The story of the two Giants, Gargantua and his son Pantagruel, fantastic as they are, is rooted in reality. Rabelais's knowledge of the Greek and Latin authors is deep and at his effortless command, but he is also aware of the patois of the unlettered. He is a connoisseur of the tales the peasants shared and passed on orally through generations. Larbaud's 'comprehensive and human' is apt. Even when the references to the politics of the period are not immediately comprehensible and require footnotes for explication, the generous sweep of the narrative carries the reader along to the next satisfyingly incredible event.

Reading *Gargantua* today, it's possible to see that Rabelais is the begetter of the picaresque novel. Like Cervantes, he is in tune with the unexpected. Nothing seems preordained or designed to a plan – the storyteller (and Rabelais is a consummate storyteller and anecdotist of the most buttonholing kind) is free to go where he wishes, taking his characters with him. The method, such as it is, ensures continuous surprise, and surprise is of the essence in such loose-limbed art. You feel, as you read, that Rabelais is delighting himself with his own conceits, but not indulgently so. He's a satirist, too, and satire is the expression of contempt for the status quo. Rabelais loved, and was intrigued by, his fellow man, but there are aspects of authority that have to be ridiculed. And not just authority, since everyday meanness – financial as well as spiritual – has to be mocked.

He makes of mankind a Giant Gargantua, and gives him a 'most horrific life' to endure. 'A soul cannot dwell in a dry place, m'lud,' remarks one of Rabelais's characters before his copious drinker, who will piss an entire river, is even born. 'The whole point of drinking is to get drunk, nezpa?'; it might be Shakespeare's Falstaff speaking. In the magical Chapter 13, the little (how 'little' is 'little'?) Gargantua tells his father Grandgousier, who has returned from his conquest of the Canarians, that 'throughout the whole land there was no boy cleaner than himself', because he has, 'by long and intensive experiments invented a means of wiping my arse'. He then lists – and Rabelais is the master of lists – the various items of ladies' accoutrements he has tried out in the interests of anal hygiene. They include a gentlewoman's 'velvet mask', a lady's kerchief and even his mother's gloves. On and on he talks, while his father laughs at the revelations of his 'little rogue'.

The whole of Chapter 22 is devoted to the games the young Gargantua plays. The list-making here takes on the form of an exhilarating poetry, with the titles of the sports and pastimes becoming ever wilder and wilder. There's 'Whirligig' and 'The cherry pit' and 'Fatarse' and 'The forked oak' and 'Fart-in-throat', among many others. But then the boy comes to manhood and his adventures begin. The best of these involves Brother John, the jovial monk who warms Gargantua's vast heart. He must rank with the rude immortals, such as Chaucer's Wife of Bath. The dedicated glutton is 'a fine dispatcher of hourly prayers, a fine dismantler of masses, a fine polisher off of vigils', not the cold ascetic of conventional wisdom. Gargantua builds for him the Abbey of Thelema, on the gate of which is an Inscription that shows Rabelais at the most scurrilously inventive.

The inhabitants of the abbey, the Thelemites, are afforded a charmed life:

> 'Their whole life was lived, not in accordance with laws, statutes or rules, but by their own choosing and free will. They got up when they felt like it; they drank, ate, worked and slept when they so desired. Nobody woke them up, nobody forced them either to drink, or to eat, or to do anything else at all. This is how Gargantua had laid it down. In their rule, there was only one clause: DO WHATEVER YOU WANT...'

The Abbey of Thelema is an earthly paradise, a vision of bliss and freedom from the anxieties of existence. It's a humanist's oasis, a chimera. The unstoppable Rabelais moves on from this place of rest, because the anxieties and misfortunes of being human are eternal. There remains only laughter to confound them.

– Paul Bailey, 2003

The entrance requirements that Rabelais's anagrammatical stand-in Alcofribas Nasier imposes on his readers are clearly set out in the opening words of the Prologue. To two categories, and to these two categories alone, are his writings dedicated: boozers, and those riddled with the pox. So unless you are a bit too fond of the bottle, or are suffering from an unmentionable disease, or (no doubt preferably both), keep out!

Of course, in times when life is being lived to the full, this admonition need not actually exclude very many people at all, especially given the elasticity of Rabelais's terms, which refer to pretty much any kind of enthusiastic sociability. And Rabelais is always playing games with inclusion and exclusion, just as he is always condemning the very same practices in which he so spectacularly indulges. He invites us into his text only to slam the door in our faces as early as Chapter 2 with the opaque enigmas of the 'Antidoted Frattlefuggs', a rhyming riddle of great antiquity discovered in a bronze tomb in Rabelais's own part of Touraine. The beginning of the document has been gnawed away by the creatures of time; what is left is an example of the genre known in French as '*coq-à-l'âne*'. It sounds even more Rabelaisian in English: 'from cock to ass' (*donkey*, that is…) – a skipping from one subject to another, often in rhyme but without any obvious reason. There's something here about licking a slipper, curing a cold with the perfume of a turnip, discussing St Patrick's hole (and other holes); various Olympian deities do a tetchy walk-on turn, and we end up with an apocalyptic prophecy of Nostradamus-like indeterminacy. All very confusing. But the gentle reader quickly pops on a pair of Aristotelian spectacles and ponders the deep meaning that may lie beneath this superficial nonsense. Is the gentle reader right to do so?

The Prologue says both 'yes' and 'no' to this. Alcofribas bids us remember Socrates, compared by Plato with a Silenus figure: repulsive and ridiculous on the outside, but full of goodness within. (This brief vignette of Socrates, as much of a Holy – or unholy – Fool as a subtle dialectician, as much the St Francis of philosophy as the donnish teaser-out of 'it all depends what you mean by…', is one of the most beautiful passages in *Gargantua*, comparable with the even more brilliant and haunting depiction of the great Cynic philosopher Diogenes of Sinope in the Prologue to Rabelais's later *Third Book*, which continues where *Gargantua* leaves off.) Maybe the text we are reading is the same – the Renaissance equivalent of knob-jokes, farts, potty humour and flatulent booziness on the outside, but containing within it 'a heavenly and priceless drug', that 'substantial marrow' sought by the most philosophical (and cynical) of beasts, the dog. But before we enthusiastically launch out into our learned exegeses, Alcofribas without warning pulls the rug away from under our feet. Do you really think – he asks – that Homer or Ovid wanted in their texts to convey the allegorical (and often moralistic) meaning that has been read into them by centuries of commentators? If you do, you're a fool, a 'Brother Boobius'. But if you *don't* – if you think that the text is already completely perspicuous, its meaning as clear as the belly of a fish floating upside down (dead) in the stream – then why does Rabelais himself insist that readers go beneath the surface to disinter a meaning that is not at first apparent? We must interpret, and yet our efforts to do so will be mocked by the text. And this is not merely a playfully aporetic manoeuvre on Rabelais's part. In his day, interpretation was a dangerous activity, theologically and (therefore) politically. He was at times *forced* to resort to the alibi of enigma if he was to scorn the objects of his hostility in relative safety; all publications ran the risk of being pored over by bureaucrats and theologians for signs of deviance from orthodoxy. Rabelaisian polysemia is not entirely the product of a freewheeling, carefree verbal exuberance, but of the need to disguise subversive and perhaps still inchoate meanings. Like Spinoza, he could have chosen as his motto the word *Caute*. Sometimes the stratagems he adopts are curiously transparent: no one would have been particularly fooled by the fact that 'theologian' in the first edition of the text was eventually replaced by 'sophist', especially given the extraordinarily detailed circumstantial evidence that survives intact to point almost unequivocally at the butt of Rabelais's scorn and anger: the reactionary and repressive Sorbonne. But Rabelais is a squid who squirts out so much ink that the satire is at times drowned out. The Antidoted Frattlefuggs may well evince suspicion of papal and imperial power, but if you fish for such straightforward meanings, you are likely to catch little more than small fry; the slippery eel will continue to lurk in the depths. Likewise, in the similar enigma that ends the work – the rhyming riddle found in the foundations of the Abbey of Thelema – the object of the description (a real battle? a theological battle? a tennis match?) is less important than the question of *scale* it raises (maybe murderous religious controversies are a mere sport: much ado about nothing). Another potentially allegorical text, *Gulliver's Travels*, draws similar effects from the counterpointing of the large and the small.

Gargantua, like all Rabelais's work, can (of course) be read as a satire; beneath the bonhomie there is quite enough savage indignation. But it can also be read as a novel. A perfectly realistic novel, too, with characters, setting, story – much more realistic than most 'Realist' novels of the last couple of centuries, being so rooted in Rabelais's own world that practically every site in the Picrocholine War can be identified as a real village, or wood, or ford, near the author's birthplace. (*Gargantua* has been hailed as the first French regional novel. It is less Parisian, and more pastoral, than *Pantagruel*.) Rabelais allots roles to real people he knew, and allows them to rub shoulders with giants and other fictions. The density of specific and compendious reference, especially to the body at its most bracingly appetitive, libidinal or excrementitious, but also to real food, games, songs, plants, birds, emblems, saints, weapons, clothes, gymnastic turns, oaths, curses and blessings would, after Rabelais, during the hegemony of French neo-classicism (with its more allusive, generalising, selective and suggestive aesthetic), go into eclipse, not to reemerge for at least three hundred years. And yet, again unlike most Realist novels, this one includes all those aspects of reality that we judge 'unreal' (or 'surreal'): the grotesque, the fantastical, the whimsical, the exaggerated, the taking of metaphors literally, the sudden inflations of local detail to cosmic significance and the equally unexpected bringing down to size of the lofty and exalted. Novelistic, too, is Rabelais's ability to identify with the object of his aggression, and see the world, for a moment, through the eyes of his enemies. His skill, for instance, at parodying the language of late scholasticism in the harangue of Master Janotus de Bragmardo, pleading for Gargantua to return the bells of Notre-Dame (Chapter 19), shows a profound knowledge of that intricate, if impractical, jargon (it's a nice touch that Janotus himself joins in the burst of laughter that greets his stuttering, rheumy, coughing, half-baked performance). Rabelais's account of the Picrocholine War is both a skit on epic (like Swift's Big-Enders versus Little-Enders, except that here the occasion is not eggs but cakes), and an example of it. Indeed, for long stretches, the writing here becomes quite straightforward: Picrochole is less of a fantasy figure than *Pantagruel*'s Werewolf and, despite the enlivening presence of Brother John of the Mincemeat (the nearest this book gets to the earlier work's Lord of Misrule, Panurge), there is a certain seriousness in the account of the war that brings it closer to real epic than to mock-epic. Thus the precise, dispassionate anatomical detail of its battle scenes, reminding us that Rabelais was, as it were, at the cutting edge of the surgery of his time, also shows us something important about what it is ostensibly parodying – how much of the *Iliad*, for instance, is (just like Rabelais's account of the exploits of Brother John), a series of close-ups of a sharp weapon entering a human body *just here* and emerging, drenched with blood, *right there* (the spear that cleaves Pandarus' nose beside the eye, shattering his white teeth, severing the tongue at the root, and smashing out through his chin, *Iliad*, Book 5).

If epic and mock-epic sometimes coincide, so do realism and the 'deeper' meanings that it seems to invite. Gargantua's livery is detailed for the purposes of realism (these are the clothes he just happened to wear) but also scrutinised for the allegorical meanings it may bear – and these meanings are in turn mocked, like the rebuses and emblems that Rabelais derides in the same section (Chapter 9). Rabelais knows that the real cannot be represented in language without the accretion, both feared and desired, of unpredictable meanings. So even the realism that he is in some ways inventing is also simultaneously being questioned. His love of lists, for instance, is a way of cataloguing the world in all its obdurate concreteness, but also of showing how impossible any such endeavour always is. The list of the games played by the young Gargantua seems so immense that it must be exhaustive – and yet it isn't, of course. All these games, played for fun, end up seeming, on the contrary, *exhausting* – not playful at all. (I have in turn occasionally played fast-and-loose with Rabelais's list of games, for various reasons, but mainly to register the sense of *panic* – a word coming from the Greek for 'all' – that such lists can induce. Rabelais would no doubt view such tampering, however minor, as worthy of the punishment he rather hypocritically metes out to the makers of tasteless homonyms on p. 27.) Likewise, the catalogue of arse-wipes invented by young Gargantua gives rise to the suspicion that everything in the world *may* well exist, as Mallarmé thought, to end up in a book, but can equally well serve to be smeared with excrement. On a different level, the excitement we feel on reading, in Chapter 33, of the vast horizons on the world opening up to Renaissance exploration is tempered by the realisation that this world is viewed by Picrochole as a mere space for his own self-aggrandisement: the world exists to be colonised. In this way, expansion and contraction follow each other, just as this earthly globe becomes, in the Thelema enigma, a tennis ball.

Thelema itself is, notoriously, less of a blueprint for utopia than it might seem. This anti-abbey is too mechanical in its inversion of the values of late medieval monasticism. Poverty, chastity and obedience are replaced by Bright Young Things disporting themselves in a kind of Summerhill-cum-Oxbridge-sur-Loire (do they really actually set foot in that lovely library?). By obsessively detailing their clothes, Rabelais turns their existence into one long fashion parade. A marriage bureau, too, since they all manage to find a mate – not surprising, given the alarming uniformity and domesticity that soon settles down on this apparently libertarian community with its celebrated anarchist motto, 'Do whatever you want'. It is disheartening to see that they all manage to want the same things at the same time. Someone says 'Let's play!' and they all play. Not for nothing was Rabelais the inventor (elsewhere in this text) of the French word *automate*. It is as if the brainchild of Brother John and Gargantua is a textbook illustration of the sociologist Max Weber's observation that once Luther had left the cloister and initiated the secularisation of the religious life, *everyone* became a monk or a nun; apparent freedom and spontaneity were merely regulated by more internalised (and thus more insidious) constraints. Still, despite the whiff of secular utilitarianism in Rabelais's anti-monasticism, there is plenty to suggest that Brother François would never have signed up to the Protestant work ethic. The humanist tutor Ponocrates may follow his student Gargantua into the lavatory so as not to lose a single moment in the work of education, but we are not obliged to follow this pedagogic practice (though, admittedly, with the right students it can pay dividends).

So the Abbey of Thelema (which after all excludes the 'poxy' characters who were welcomed by the Prologue) is not an ending. After *Gargantua*, Rabelais will embark his characters on yet further adventures – in the *Third Book*, the *Fourth Book* and the largely apocryphal *Fifth Book* – that always seem to remain open-ended, perpetually 'to be continued'. Nor is it a utopia; perhaps no *place* can be a utopia, even if language can intimate utopian communities – the boozers celebrating Gargantua's birth in Chapter 5, for instance, which gives you the (not entirely illusory) sense of hearing directly the real voices of people carousing for all their worth at a party held fifteen generations ago. *Gargantua* itself ends with a riddling shrug – but not before its hero has grown from leaky baby to mature Renaissance man, tyrants have been defeated, and the straw men of the established order have been held up for mocking inspection. And, as important as any of these, we have been allowed to share the bantering exchanges of a crowd at a nativity scene. When Erasmus retranslated the opening words of St John's Gospel into Latin, he deviated from the Vulgate version *In principio erat verbum* and replaced it with *In principio erat sermo* – to be charged, inevitably, with heresy. He meant many things by *sermo*, but one of them, surely, was simply 'speech'. In the beginning was, not merely a metaphysical Logos or a hypostasised abstraction, but human speech – the speech of boozy babble and idle gossip, the speech that floods Rabelais's writing: the speech of human beings gabbling away since the foundations of the world.

– Andrew Brown, 2003

Note on the Text:

My translation is based on the critical edition of Rabelais's *Cinq livres* by Jean Céard, Gérard Defaux and Michel Simonin (Paris: Livre de Poche, Librairie Générale Française, 1994), which incorporates Rabelais's final revisions. My notes are almost entirely from this edition.

This translation, for all its imperfections, is dedicated with love to Jenny, Adam, Rachel and Matthew, who have taught me even more about laughter (and potty-training) than did Rabelais.

Gargantua

TO THE READER

My friends who are about to read this book,
Rid yourselves of all prejudice as you read,
And do not here for harm or scandal look,
You'll find nothing to shock you. Yes indeed,
There's nothing here to which you must pay heed,
Except this lesson: laughter's good for you.
And that's the best of arguments, since few
Advantages come from the grief and sorrow
That harass you. Writing should laugh, not weep,
Since laughter is of man the very marrow.

LIVE IN JOY

Most distinguished boozers, and you, most dearly beloved pox-sufferers (it is to you, and no one else, that my writings are dedicated), Alcibiades, in Plato's dialogue called *The Symposium*, praising his teacher Socrates, who was without any question the prince of philosophers, among other things describes him as being similar to Sileni. Sileni were, in bygone days, little boxes, of the same kind we see these days in the shops of apothecaries, painted on the outside with joyful, frivolous figures, such as harpies, satyrs, bridled goslings, horned hares, saddled ducks, flying goats, harnessed stags, and other such paintings designed expressly for the pleasure of making everyone laugh. Such a character was Silenus, the master of the good Bacchus. But inside, they preserved fine drugs, such as balm, ambergris, amomum, musk, civet and precious stones, and other things of great value. Such, Alcibiades said, was Socrates, because, seeing him from the outside, and judging him on his external appearance, you wouldn't have given the shred of an onion skin for him, he was so physically ugly, and had such a ridiculous bearing, with his snub nose, his eyes like a bull's, and the face of a madman. He behaved like a simpleton, wore shabby clothes, was poor in fortune, unlucky with women, no good for any of the offices of the republic; always laughing, always matching anyone drink for drink, always blathering, always concealing his divine knowledge. But on opening this box, you'd have found inside a heavenly and priceless drug: a more than human understanding, a wonderful virtue, an invincible courage, an unparalleled sobriety, an unshakeable contentment, a perfect self-assurance and an incredible scorn for all that makes humans lose so much sleep, and all that they run, labour, sail the seas and fight battles to gain.

What, in your opinion, is the purpose and aim of this prelude and preliminary essay? Well, it's because you, my faithful disciples, and a few other idle fools, reading the merry titles of some books of our invention, such as *Gargantua*, *Pantagruel*, *Tosspint*, *On the Dignity of Codpieces*, *Peas with Bacon* (annotated edition),[1] etc., decide too hastily that in them there can't be anything more than wicked japes, droll quips and merry pranks. After all, the outward sign (i.e. the title), if you don't bother to enquire any further, is commonly taken as evidence of hilarity and ribald jokes within. But you shouldn't judge human works so lightly. You yourselves say that the habit doesn't make the monk; and there's many a one who wears a monk's habit, but inside is anything but a monk; and many a one who wears a Spanish cape, who has none of the courage we associate with Spain. That's why you have to open the book and carefully weigh what is set out in it. Then you'll realise that the drug it contains is of a far different value from what the box seemed to promise. That is, the subject matter discussed inside is not quite so frolicsome as the title on the outside suggested.

And, even supposing that on the literal level you find subject matter that's perfectly merry and fully lives up to the book's name, nonetheless you mustn't stop there – as if listening to the sirens' song – but interpret in a higher sense what you may well have thought was merely said out of gaiety of heart.

Did you ever pick the lock of the wine cupboard and swipe a few bottles? You old dogs! Try and think back to the expression you had on your face. But did you ever see a dog coming across some marrow bone? The dog is – according to Plato (*The Republic*, Book 2) – the most philosophical creature in the world. If you've ever seen one, you'll have noted how devotedly he watches over it, how carefully he guards it, how fervently he holds it, how cautiously he makes a start on it, how affectionately he breaks it open, and how diligently he sucks it. What induces him to do this? What does he hope to gain by his zeal? What good does he imagine he will attain? Nothing more than a little marrow. True, this little marrow is more delicious than a great quantity of other things he might eat, since marrow is that food which is refined to natural perfection, as Galen says (*Natural Faculties*, Book 3, and *The Functions of the Parts of the Body*, Book 11).

Following this example, you should have the flair to sniff out, smell out and assess these lovely and most excellent books, to be swift in pursuit and bold in the encounter. Then, reading them closely and attentively, and meditating on them frequently, you should break the bone and suck out the substantial marrow – i.e. what I am getting at, by means of these Pythagorean symbols – in the certain hope of being made more shrewd and valorous as you read. You will find quite

4

another taste to it, and a more recondite meaning, which will reveal to you some most holy sacraments and horrific mysteries, both in the things that concern our religion, and in politics and economics.

Do you really believe, in your heart of hearts, that Homer, writing the *Iliad* and the *Odyssey*, ever thought of the allegories that he has been lumbered with by Plutarch, Heraclides Ponticus, Eustathius and Cornutus, not to mention the ones that Poliziano pinched from all of them?

If you do believe this, well, you're still miles away from my own opinion, which decrees that they were as little thought of by Homer as the sacraments of the Gospel were dreamt of by Ovid in his *Metamorphoses* – though a certain Brother Boobius, a real bacon-filcher, has contrived to demonstrate just this, on the off-chance that he might come across people as crazy as himself and (as the proverb puts it) a cover worthy of the pot.[2]

If you *don't* believe it – well, what reason is there for you to believe these merry and brand-new chronicles? After all, while I was dictating them, I didn't bother my head about them any more than did you, who were perhaps drinking just as heavily as I was. And while I was dictating this most lordly book, I didn't waste any time on it other than the time designated for my bodily refection, i.e. for eating and drinking. That is, after all, exactly the right time for setting down these lofty matters, this deep learning. Homer, that paragon of all philologists, was a past master in the art, as was Ennius, the father of Latin poets, witness Horace – though one dunderhead has said that his songs reeked of wine rather than oil.

Some suspect monkish character says exactly the same thing about *my* books, but shit on him! The aroma of wine, ah! how much more mouth-watering, laughter-inducing and alluring it is, more heavenly and delicious than oil! And I'll glory just as much if people say of me that I spent more on wine than on oil, as did Demosthenes when people said of him that he spent more on oil than on wine.[3] I reckon it is nothing but honour and glory to have the reputation of being called a real joker and jolly good company, and under this name I am welcome in all good assemblies of Pantagruelists. One old grouch criticised Demosthenes for the fact that his orations smelt like the rag of a dirty, filthy oil-seller. And so you should interpret all my deeds and words in the most charitable way; revere the cheesy brain that is feeding you with these lovely little loony tales; and, to the best of your abilities, always keep me company, all merry and bright!

And so just put your feet up, my loves, and merrily read the rest, for your body's ease and the solace of your kidneys! But listen, too, you donkey pizzles – may blotches and blains cover you from head to foot! – just you remember to drink my health in return, and I'll raise a toast to you this very minute!

CHAPTER 1
The genealogy and antiquity of Gargantua

You can check out the great Pantagrueline Chronicle to remind your-selves of the genealogy and antiquity from which Gargantua came to us. In it, you'll find a more detailed account of how the Giants were born in this world, and how from them, by a direct line of descent, sprang Gargantua, Pantagruel's father; and you won't mind too much if I don't go into it just now – even though it's one of those matters that, the more you're reminded of it, the more your lordships will take pleasure in it. You have it on Plato's authority in the *Philebus* and the *Gorgias*, and Horace too, who says that there are certain stories, just like these ones no doubt, that are the more delightful the more often they are repeated. Would to God that everyone could know his genealogy with just as much certainty, from Noah's Ark down to the present! I believe that many who today are emperors, kings, dukes, princes and popes, throughout the world, are in fact descended from pedlars of relics and carriers of hods. Likewise, there are several hospice inmates, poor suffering wretches, who are descended from the blood and lineage of great kings and emperors, given the amazing way that kingdoms and empires have been transferred – from the Assyrians to the Medes, the Medes to the Persians, the Persians to the Macedonians, the Macedonians to the Romans, the Romans to the Greeks, the Greeks to the French.

And so you can hear a little about yours truly, let me tell you I'm sure I'm descended from some rich king or prince of bygone times. Why? Because you've never seen any fellow with a greater hankering to be a king, and a rich man, than me. Then I could really live it up, and not do a tap of work, and have not a care in the world, and lavish treats on my friends and all decent, well-educated fellows. But I take comfort from the fact that in the next world I *will* be rich; yes, and even richer than I could ever hope to be in the present. And if you're feeling down in the dumps, take comfort from the same thought, or an even more alluring one, and have a nice cool drink if you can.

Returning to my main point, I'm glad to tell you that by the sovereign gift of the heavens, the antiquity and genealogy of Gargantua has been preserved for us, in a greater state of completeness than any other – apart

7

from that of the Messiah, which I'd rather leave out of this, as I have no right to talk about it, and the devils (i.e. the slanderers and zealots) would object. This genealogy was found by Jean Audeau, in a meadow he owned near the Gualeau Arch, below the *Olive* on the way to Narsay.[4] The ditches were being turned over, and the diggers' little picks struck a great bronze tomb, immeasurably long – so long that they never found the end of it, as it extended too far into the mill dams of the River Vienne. Opening it up – just below the place where it was embossed with a goblet, around which was written in Etruscan letters HIC BIBITVR[5] – they found nine flagons, arranged in the same way as ninepins are set out in Gascony. The one in the middle stood on top of a huge, fat, large, grey, attractive, little, mouldy book, smelling stronger but not better than roses. In it, the genealogy I mentioned was found, written out at length in chancery letters, not on paper, not on parchment, not on wax, but on elm bark; but these letters were so worn with age that it was almost impossible to make out three in a row.

I, unworthy though I be, was summoned over, so I popped on my specs and, applying the art of reading invisible letters as taught by Aristotle, I transcribed it, as you'll see if you Pantagruelise, in other words drink as much as you want while reading the horrific deeds of Pantagruel. At the end of the book there was a short treatise entitled *The Antidoted Frattlefuggs*. The rats and cockroaches or (I don't want to tell a fib now, do I?) maybe some other nasty little beasties had gnawed the beginning away; the rest I have included below, out of reverence for antiquity.

CHAPTER 2
The Antidoted Frattlefuggs, discovered in an ancient monument

...who m/de the Cimbri yield,[6]
...-ing through air, for fear of all the dew,
...his coming, all the troughs they quickly filled,
...a great shower of butter fresh and new,
...grandma that yellow liquid did imbue,
She cried aloud, 'for mercy's sake, mein Herr,

Fish him out quick, his beard's all covered in pooh,
Or leastways offer him a nice long ladder!'

Some said, 'It's better far to lick his slipper
Than for our wicked sins pardons to poach.'
Along there came a foppish little nipper
Straight from the pond where they all fish for roach,
Who said, 'Chaps, no! lest we incur reproach:
Just look, it really couldn't be any clearer –
That eel that in the depths all day does lurk
Has a great stain down there on his tiara.'

He was about to read out the next chapter
But all that he could see were a calf's horns.
'I feel,' he said, 'cold all around my mitre,
So dreadfully cold it chills my very brains.'
A turnip's perfume soon his ailment mends;
He is content to huddle by the hearth;
So long as a new courser someone sends
To folks who are a little short on mirth.

All they could talk of was St Patrick's hole,
Gibraltar, and some other deep holes too:
If anyone could deign to make them whole
So that their nasty cough away would go…
It seemed to all that, when the wind would blow,
They'd get into a quite impertinent tizz
Unless they were so very tightly closed
That they could be delivered as hostages.

By this decree they had him skin the crow –
Old Hercules, come straight from Libya.
'What's this?' said Minos. 'Why can't I come too?
Everyone but me gets an invite to dinner!
And they expect me to suppress my inner
Desire to provide some oysters and nice frogs!

The devil take them all! No, I shall never
Have mercy on the way they sold those logs.'

Up limped Q.B. ... You know – old Hopalong.
Safe conduct for the starlings that arose
In mystic flight he sought. Sifter, the strong
Cyclops' cousin slew them. Blow your nose,
All people! No, he wasn't one of those,
Though some there were who mocked him in the mill.
Sound the alarm! A tear in every nose!
You did not have much then: one day, you will.

Shortly thereafter, Jupiter's great bird
Laid bets not on the best but on the worst.
But seeing them all so shaken and so stirred
He feared they'd lay the empire in the dust.
He'd rather see them fire from heaven wrest
From that old tree-trunk where you can buy herrings,
Than that air, 'gainst which we conspire the most,
Should be subject to Masoretic writings.

All this was made in every detail clear,
Despite the goddess Até with her thigh
Of heron, who when she saw Penthesilea
In her old age thought she was shouting, 'Buy
My cress!' And everyone cried out, 'You sly
Old collier's wife, who wants you for a neighbour?
You pinched that great and lofty Roman banner
That had been written on fine-quality paper!'

Neither was Juno from her heavenly height
With her fierce owl laying a fearsome snare:
She would have been in a most dreadful plight,
Her clothes suffering from terrible wear and tear.
The pact was made; her fare for this affair
Would be two eggs from fair Persephone.

If ever she was found in bondage there,
They'd tie her to a mountain hawthorn tree.

Seven months went by, minus some twenty-two,
When he who once annihilated Carthage
Courteously sat among that motley crew
Requesting they accept his heritage:
Or else they could share out, if they could manage,
The goods, following the law they'd all agreed;
And they could dole out such a mess of pottage
To all those cads who had drawn up the deed.

The year will come, signed with a Turkish bow
With spindles five and scrapings from the pot
That a discourteous king will be laid low
By pox scabs hidden beneath his gown of hermit.
It's pitiful! For such a hypocrite
To let yourselves be swallowed by several acres?…
No one can mimic such a mummer. Stop it!
Go back to old snake's bro, that King of Fakers.

When that year's gone by, He Who Is shall reign
In peace with all his friends and all his allies.
There'll be no tumult then, and no more pain;
Men of good will shall have their compromise.
And all the solace that of yore was promised
To all heaven's dwellers will come to his belfry.
The stud farms that were then so much astonished
Will triumph on their proud and royal palfrey.

And then this time of jugglers' feints and passes
Will last till we from Mars can gain release.
Then one shall come… all others he surpasses
Handsome, delightful, pleasant to excess.
Lift up your hearts in longing for this peace,
My faithful friends. A man whose day is done

Would really rather stay dead and deceased,
So loud the clamour for the time that's gone.

And finally, the man who was of wax
Will lodgings find next to the hinges loud,
No longer 'Lord, Lord', no more bending backs
To any gonging dong that keeps men cowed.
Ha, who could then draw out his trusty sword?
They'd be no more, the nets that worry weaves:
And we could clean out, with a thread that's broad
And strong, this hucksters' mall, this den of thieves.

CHAPTER 3
How Gargantua was carried in his mother's womb for eleven months

Grandgousier was a real barrel of laughs in his day; he loved to booze, as much as any other man of that time, and he was very fond of salty food. So he usually made sure he had a good supply of ham from Mainz and Bayonne, plenty of smoked oxtongues, an abundance of chitterlings when they were in season, and salt beef with mustard. Loads of botargo, and heaps of sausages, though not the Bologna sort, as he'd heard about the kinds of things that go into Lombardy titbits – instead, those from Bigorre, Longaulnay, La Brenne and Rouargue.

Having reached man's estate he married Gargamelle, daughter of the King of the Flutterbies[7], a pretty lass with a nice phiz. And the two of them frequently played the beast with two backs, merrily rubbing their bacon together, until in the end she got pregnant with a fine baby boy, and carried him until the eleventh month.

Women can carry that long, you know, and even longer, especially when it's some great masterpiece they're hatching, a personage who in his time is destined to perform heroic deeds. So Homer says that when Neptune got a nymph pregnant, the child was born a whole year later: twelve full months. As Aulus Gellius says (Book 3), this long term befitted the majesty of Neptune, so that the child would have time to grow to perfection. For a similar reason, Jupiter made the night he slept with Alcmene last forty-eight hours. If he'd taken any less time, he'd never have been able to create Hercules, who cleansed the world of monsters and tyrants.

The distinguished old Pantagruelists have confirmed my words and declared as not only possible, but also legitimate, the child born from the woman in the eleventh month after her husband's death. Hippocrates in *De alimento*, or *Food*; Pliny in Book 7, Chapter 5; Plautus in *Cistellaria*, or *The Casket*; Marcus Varro, in the satire called *The Testament*, where he relies on the authority of Aristotle; Censorinus, *De die natali*, or *The Day of Birth*; Aristotle, Book 7, Chapters 3 and 4, *De nat. animalium*, or *The Nature of Animals*; Gellius, Book 3, Chapter 16; Servius, *In Egl.*, or *On the Eclogues*, in his note on Virgil's line '*Matri longa decem*', etc.; and a thousand other lunatics, whose numbers have been swelled by the lawyers, *ff. De suis & legit., l. Intestato, §* fi. And in *Autent. De restitut. & ea quae parit in .xi. mens*, or *The Legitimacy of a Child Born to a Woman in Her 11th Month*. What's more, they've stuffed their bacon-bumping law full of passages from Gallus, *ff de lib. et posthu.*, and *l. Septimo. ff. de stat. homini*, and several others, which for the present I dare not name.[8] By means of laws such as these, widows can play rumpy-pumpy to their hearts' content, as and when they will, two months after their husband's death. So, all you jokers out there, do me a favour: if you ever come across any who are worth getting your flies undone for, climb on top of them and bring them along to me. After all, if they get pregnant in the third month, their offspring will be the heir of the late lamented. And once their pregnancy is known, they can really let their hair down and have a ball, since their belly is already full. Julia, the Emperor Octavian's daughter, never abandoned herself to her Mr Tambourine Men unless she felt she was pregnant, just as the boat never takes on its pilot unless it's first been caulked and loaded. And if anyone criticises them for getting themselves ratacuntarsed like this while they're up the duff, seeing that pregnant animals can't stand having males moiling and toiling on *their* fat bellies, the women reply that that's the animals' problem; *they* are women, and fully aware of the fine and dandy details of their rights of superfetation – as Popilia replied, according to Macrobius, *Saturnalia,* Book 2.[9]

If the devil doesn't want them to get pregnant, they'll just have to shut the spigot and hang up a sign saying 'closed'.

CHAPTER 4
How Gargamelle, while pregnant with Gargantua, ate a great quantity of tripes

Gargamelle gave birth in the following way, and if you don't believe me, may your bumgut drop out! Her bumgut fell out after dinner on the 4th February, as a result of her eating too many godebillioes. Godebillioes are the fat tripes of coiroes. Coiroes are cattle fatted in the manger, and in guimo fields. Guimo fields are those that grow grass twice a year.[10] Of these fat oxen, 367,014 had been slaughtered to be salted at Shrovetide, so that all through the spring they would have heaps of beef in season, and could make a brief commemoration of salty food at the start of their meals, and then relish their wine more. The tripes were plentiful, as you can imagine, and so delicious that everyone was left licking his fingers from them. But the devil of it all was that they couldn't be preserved for long: they'd have gone off. And this seemed deplorable. So it was decided that they'd fill their faces with these tripes and not waste a single morsel. With this aim in view, they invited all the townsfolk of Sinay, Seuillé, La Roche Clermauld and Vaugaudry, without forgetting Le Coudray Montpensier, the Gué de Vède and other neighbouring towns: all good boozers, good company and good skittle players.

Mine host Grandgousier was delighted to see it, and ordered oodles of everything to be served up. He did suggest to his wife, however, that she shouldn't eat as much as anyone else, since she was near her time, and this tripe was, well, a load of tripe – not really the nicest kind of meat. Anyone who eats a sackful of this stuff, he said, would be just as happy eating shite. But in spite of these warnings, she ate sixteen hogsheads, two bushels and six pecks' worth. O fine faecal fare, that was soon to swell up inside her!

After dinner, they all went pell-mell to the willow grove, and there, on the thick grass, they danced to the sound of the merry flageolets and sweet bagpipes, and enjoyed themselves so much that it warmed the cockles of your heart to see them having such heavenly fun.

CHAPTER 5
The conversations of the comboozelated

Then they started to talk about dessert, which they took in the same place. And flagons started going round, hams trotted by, goblets flew along, and jugs started clinking.

'Draw one for me! Come on, over here! Turn the tap on! I'll have mine mixed.'

'Pour it out!'

'I'll have mine neat!'

'That's right, mate… Go on, fill 'er up, there's a good chap!'

'A glass of claret please!'

'Right to the top!'

'That's the last of the thirst!'

'Phew! I'm all hot and bothered. I could do with a drink.'

'Gawd Ormidey, ducky, I cahd zeeb do zwallow id.'

'Got a cold, 'ave yer?'

'Yesh.'

'By the belly of St Quim! Now *that's* what I call a drink!'

'*I* only drink when I feel like it, just like the Pope's mule.'

'*I* only drink in my breviary, like a good reverend.'

'Which came first, thirst or drinking?'

'Thirst came first. Who'd have ever drunk without being thirsty during the time of innocence?'

'No, drinking. *Privatio presupponit habitum*,[11] as they say. Ooh, aren't I a cleverclogs!'

'*Faecundi calices quem non fecere disertum?*'[12]

'Us other innocent folks can drink all too well without feeling thirsty.'

'Not me. I'm a sinner, I'm not thirsty, at least not now, but I *will* be, so I drink in anticipation – get my drift? I drink for my thirst to come. I drink eternally. Oh, an eternity of drinking, and drinking to all eternity!'

'Wine, women and song! Come on, let's have a song!'

'No, let's have a swig.'

'Looks like my friends are doing my drinking for me.'

'Do you get sloshed so you can dry out, or do you dry out so you can get sloshed?'

'Hm, I don't know. That's a difficult one in theory. Let's stick to practice…'

'Hurry up!'

'I wet my whistle, I irrigate my tonsils, I – drink! And all because I'm scared of dying. Don't stop drinking, and you'll never die!'

'If I don't drink, I get all dry. And then I die. My soul flies off to some frog pond. A soul cannot dwell in a dry place, m'lud.'

'Wine waiters, you creators of new forms, turn me from a teetotaller to a total teeterer!'

'Keep my parched and twisted innards permanently nice and wet!'

'The whole point of drinking is to get drunk, nezpa?'

'This stuff is going straight into my veins, and there won't be a drop left to siphon the python.'

'I'd really like to wash the tripes of that calf I dressed this morning.'

'I've ballasted my stomach pretty well.'

'If the paper of my bills drank as well as I do, my creditors would get their wine all right, and there'd be no evidence to show the judge.'

'Raise your glass and ruin your nose.'

'Oh, how many other glasses of wine will go in before this one comes out!'

'I'm going to bust a gut if I have to lean down to drink from such shallow waters!'

'This flagon is like a rat-trap for the rat-arsed.'

'What's the difference between a bottle and a flagon?'

'All the difference in the world! A bottle is stopped with a cork, and a flagon is like a certain little hole, you just put a bung in it.'

'Our fathers drank deep and drained their glasses to the very last drop.'

'Oh, what a shitty, whoops, I mean witty fellow. Time for another one!'

'Got any tripes you want washing in the river? Yours truly will wash them in wine.'

'I drink like a Templar.'

'And I *tanquam sponsus*.'

'And I *sicut terra sine aqua*.'[13]

'What's the definition of "ham"?'

'It's a puller of drinks. Or rather, it's a pulley. You use a pulley to lower wine into the cellar, and you use ham to lower wine into the stomach.'

'Well, then, fill 'er up, come on! Right to the top! *Respice personam; pone pro duos; bus non est in usu.*[14]

'If I could climb as high as the drink dives down, I'd be, ooh, as high as a kite!'

'This made Jacques Coeur a very rich fellow.'[15]

'That's the advantage of keeping woods fallow.'

'Thus did Bacchus conquer India.'

'Thus spake the great philosopher Melinda.'[16]

'A little rain a day keeps the big wind away.'

'Drink all the time and you'll ward off the thunder.'

'But if my prick really produced piss like that, would *you* want to suck it?'

'I'll reserve my judgement on that one.'

'Come on, garçon! Another glass!'

'I'll insinuate my nomination to you in turn.'

'Drink up, Guillot! There's a whole jugful left.'

'I'm appealing against thirst. It's a fundamental abuse. Garçon, draw up my appeal in all due legal form!'

'Hey, is this all I get?'

'Once upon a time I'd drink it all up; now I don't leave a single drop.'

'More haste, less speed! Let's see how much is left. Look, there's some prize tripes, and godebillioes to die for, from that fawn-coloured ox with the black stripe. Oh my, Lord above! – beef curry flavour, just the thing to curry favour!'

'Drink, or I'll…'

'No, I won't.'

'Please drink!'

'Sparrows won't eat unless you tap them on the tails. And I won't drink unless you give me a cuddle.'

'*Lagona edatera!*[17] There's not a rabbit-hole in my whole body where this wine can't ferret out thirst.'

'This wine will suss it out.'

'And this one will send it packing for good.'

'Let's announce it loud and clear, to the sound of flagons and bottles: anyone who's lost his thirst won't find it here! Long clysters of drinking have thrown it out of house and home.'

'God Almighty made the planets spin and we lick the plates clean.'

'I have the Word of God in my mouth: *Sitio.*'[18]

'The stone called ἄσβεστος[19] is not more inextinguishable than the thirst of my paternity!'

'Appetite comes with eating, as Hangest of Le Mans[20] used to say; thirst goes away with drinking.'

'What's the best remedy against thirst? The opposite of the remedy used against a dog's bite. Keep running after the dog, and he'll never bite you; keep drinking before you get thirsty, and you'll never get thirsty.'

'I've caught you at it. Wakey-wakey! Eternal wine waiter, don't wait to wake us! Argus had a hundred eyes to see; a wine waiter needs a hundred hands, like Briareus, to keep pouring it out without ever tiring.'[21]

'Hey, lubrication needed here! We're all dried out!'

'A drop of white! Pour it out! Come on, devil take you, keep pouring! Come on, right to the top. My tongue's peeling!'

'*Trink*, Hans!'

'Cheers, mate! Down the hatch! Ah, that's the stuff!'

'Slips down nice and easily, it does.'

'Oh, lachryma Christi!'

'It's from La Devinière[22] – a real drop of the best!'

'Oh yes, a nice quaffing white wine – my word, very smooth for a *vin ordinaire.*'

'Yes, and there's something in it for a finer palate too: smooth, a hint of wool, I'm getting velvet…'

'Cheer up, lad! No need to pinch anything in this game, just bottoms up!'

'*Ex hoc in hoc.*[23] Nah, no need to cast a spell, you all saw it; I'm a past master at it!'

'Past? Pissed, you mean!'

'Ahem, ahem! Not pissed in the least, just a priest in the lists.'

'Oh, what a lot of boozers! What a lot of thirsty throats!'

'Garçon, my friend, just fill 'er up, and give this wine the victor's cup.'

'Red for the Cardinal!'

'*Natura abhorret vacuum.*'[24]

'Would you say a fly had been taking little sips here?'

'Breton style!'

'Vino, please! No water, thank you!'

'Swallow it down now. Just what the doctor ordered!'

CHAPTER 6
Gargantua's very strange birth

As they were chatting away over their drinks, Gargamelle started to feel a bit unwell down below. So Grandgousier stood up from where he was sitting on the grass, and started to cheer her up and say encouraging things, as he guessed it must be her labour pains, telling her she'd put herself out to graze under the willow grove, and that she'd soon be hearing the patter of little feet (and that she'd soon be back on *hers*), so she just needed to take heart at the arrival of her baby; true, the delivery might be just a tiny bit painful, but never mind, it would all be over soon, and the ensuing joy would completely outweigh the passing discomfort, and she wouldn't remember a thing. 'Make like a ewe,' he kept saying, 'and buck up! Get this one out quick and let's make another one soon!'

'Ha! Typical man! It's easy enough for *you* to talk,' she said. 'Well, anyway, for God's sake I'll try my best, since that's what you want. But I wish to God you'd chopped it off.'

'What?' said Grandgousier.

'Oh, come off it, you're having me on. *You* know what I mean.'

'My willy?' said he. 'Fine. By Old Horny, if you think it's a good idea, bring me a knife!'

'Oh, God forbid!' she said. 'God forgive me! I was kidding. Don't take me seriously, and don't even think about it! But I've got a hard time ahead of me today, unless God helps me, and it's the fault of your willy and all the pleasure it gave you!'

'Don't worry about a thing,' said he, 'it's going to be fine. Just lie back and enjoy the ride. I'm just going to pop off for another quick one. If you start to feel poorly while I'm gone, I won't be far away. Just put your hands together and give a little whistle, I'll be there like a shot.'

Shortly after, she began to heave sighs and utter lamentations and cries. Immediately, midwives came pouring in from every direction. They felt her down below and found a few lumps of rather unappetising dirty matter, and thought it must be the baby; but it was bumgut dropping out, as a result of the loosening of the right intestine, which you call the back passage; all because she'd been eating too many tripes, as we mentioned above. Whereupon a filthy old bag in the company who had the reputation of being a great doctor, and had come here from Brizepaille near Saint-Genou sixty years ago, made for her an astringent that was so horrible that all her sphincters became so contracted and tightened that it would have taken a real effort for you to have pulled them open with your teeth – which is a really horrible thought; in the same way as the devil, when he was writing down the jabberings of two French lasses at St Martin's Mass, used his big strong teeth to stretch out his parchment.[25]

This impediment meant that the upper cotyledons of the womb were loosened. The baby pushed his way up through them, and entered the vena cava, and, climbing via the diaphragm right up to the shoulders (where the said vein divides in two), he took a left turn and came out through the left ear.

The minute he was born, he didn't cry, 'Wah! Wah! Wah!' like other children. But he started shouting at the top of his lungs, 'Drink! Drink! Drink!' as if he were inviting everybody to have a drink. And he was so loud that he was heard throughout the land of Bevvy and Boozup.

I suspect you're not going to entirely believe this strange nativity. If you don't believe it, I can't say I'm particularly bothered – but a good man, a man of common sense, always believes what people tell him, and whatever he finds written down. Is it against our law, our faith, against reason, against the Holy Scriptures? For my part, I can't find anything written in the Holy Bible that speaks against it. But if it had been God's will, would you say he couldn't have done it? Ah, for mercy's sake, don't ever go jumblejambling your minds with those vain thoughts.

Let me tell you this: with God nothing shall be impossible. And if he so willed, all women would from now on give birth to their children through their ears. Wasn't Bacchus engendered through Jupiter's thigh? Wasn't Rocksplitter born from his mother's heel? Wasn't Flycruncher born from his nurse's slipper? Wasn't Minerva born from Jupiter's brain, via his ear? Adonis out of the bark of a myrrh tree? Castor and Pollux from the shell of an egg laid and hatched by Leda? But you'd be even more gobsmacked and flabbergasted if I now set out the whole of Pliny's chapter which discusses strange and unnatural births. And yet I'm not such a lying hound as he was. Read the seventh book of his *Natural History*, Chapter 3, and stop dunning my brains.[26]

CHAPTER 7
How Gargantua was given his name;
and how he enjoyed his first sniff of wine

Good old Grandgousier, knocking it back and joshing with his mates, heard the horrible cry his son had uttered as he came into the light of this world, bellowing and demanding, 'Drink! Drink! Drink!' It made him say, '*Que grand tu as*: what a big one you've got' – viz., a big mouth. On hearing this, those present said that he really ought to take 'Gargantua' as his name, since this had been his father's first word at his birth, in imitation of the example of the ancient Hebrews. Grandgousier went along with the idea, and the mother was very pleased with it too.

And to calm him down they let him drink like a fish, and he was carried to the font, and there baptised, as is the custom of all good Christian folk. And they ordered for him 17,913 cows from Pautille and Bréhémond, and this was just for his normal milk. Finding a wet nurse who could produce enough wasn't possible, anywhere in the country, considering the huge quantity of milk required to feed him. Though a few Scotist theologians *have* claimed that his mother did actually feed him herself, and that she could draw from her breasts 1,402 great casks and nine pots of milk each time. This just isn't credible. Indeed, the proposition was declared mammarously scandalous by the Sorbonne, offensive to the ears of humble believers, and with a whiff of heresy you could smell a mile off.[27]

In this state he remained, until the age of one year and ten months, when, on the doctors' orders, they started to carry him about, and a fine ox cart was made for him, designed by Jean Denyau[28]. In this they would take him out and about, all very merrily, and it was wonderful to see him, as he had a lovely little mug, and almost eighteen chins; and he didn't cry much, but he *would* keep shitting himself, being incredibly phlegmatic in the bottom department, both because of his natural complexion, and also because of the accidental disposition that he had contracted due to drinking too much autumnal liquor. And he always had a good reason for drinking. If he happened to be cross, angry, annoyed or fed up; and if he stamped his feet, cried or yelled, they'd bring him a drink and restore his spirits, and he immediately calmed down and brightened up.

One of his nannies told me, on her word of honour, that he was so used to doing this that, merely at the sound of pint pots and flagons, he would go into an ecstatic trance, as if he were tasting the delights of heaven. As a result, they took advantage of this divine disposition, and in the morning, to make him cheerful, they would make the glasses ring with a knife in front of him, or make the flagons chime with their stopper, or the pint pots with their lid. At the sound of all this, his face would brighten, he would leap with joy, and he would rock himself to and fro, nodding his head, playing a single-stringed fiddle on his fingers, and thunderfarting like a big booming bass.

CHAPTER 8
Gargantua's clothes

As he had now reached the right age, his father ordered them to make up some clothes in his own livery, which was white and blue. So they set to work, and the clothes were made, cut and sewn in the way that was then current. From the old documents in the Chamber of Accounts at Montsoreau, I find that he was dressed in the following way.

For his shirt, they used nine hundred ells of Châtellerault linen, and two hundred for the gussets, that were diamond-shaped and fitted under the armpits. And the shirt wasn't gathered, since the fashion for gathering shirts was invented only once seamstresses, when the sharp end of their needle got broken, started using their bottom ends.

For his doublet, they used 813 ells of white satin, and for the points 1,509½ dogskins. Then everyone began to attach the breeches to the doublet, and not the doublet to the breeches, which is quite unnatural, as Occam-made fully clear in his commentary on the *Exposables* of M. Highbreech.[29]

For his breeches, they used 1,105⅓ ells of white worsted. And they were slashed lengthways, like fluted columns, and crenellated behind, so as not to overheat his kidneys. And within each slash there was a fluffy gathering of blue damask, just as much as was needed. He had very handsome legs, you see, well proportioned to his overall build.

For the codpiece, they used 16¼ ells of the same fabric, and it was shaped like a flying buttress, and – a nice touch, this – fastened with two beautiful gold buckles, fitted with two enamel hooks, in each of which was set a huge emerald as big as an orange. The reason for this was that (as Orpheus says in his *Liber de lapidibus*, or *Stones*, and Pliny in his last book) emerald has an erective and stimulant effective on the male member.[30] The tail of the codpiece was as long as a piece of cane, slashed in the same way as the breeches, and also provided with floating blue damask. But if you'd seen the lovely gold embroidery, and the delightful interlaced braid adorned with fine diamonds, fine rubies, fine turquoises, fine emeralds and Persian pearls, you'd have compared it with a beautiful cornucopia of the kind you see in antique shops, and like the one Rhea gave to the two nymphs Adrastea and Ida, Jupiter's wet nurses.[31] It was always a heart-warming sight, succulent and moist, always verdant, always blooming, always fructifying, full of sap, full of blossom, full of fruit, full of all delights. Ah, I swear to God, what a wonderful thing it was to see! But I'll provide you with a more detailed account in the book I've written *On the Dignity of Codpieces*. For now, there's one thing I'd like to point out: if it was long and very substantial in size, this was because it was properly filled out and more than adequately victualled on the inside, and in no way resembled the hypocritical codpieces of a whole host of fancypants poseurs, which are full of nothing but wind, to the great disadvantage of the feminine sex.

For his shoes they used 406 ells of blue crimson velvet, and they were slashed with parallel lines joined in uniform cylinders, most elegantly. For the soles, they used 1,100 hides from brown cows, cut in codtail shape.

For his coat they used 1,800 ells of blue velvet, dyed in the grain, embroidered all around with fine ornamental borders, and down the middle with silver pint pots picked out in silver thread, interwoven with gold rings and many pearls, denoting by this that he would see off a good number of pints in his lifetime.

His belt was 300½ ells of silk serge, half white and half blue, unless I'm very much mistaken.

His sword was not from Valence, nor his dagger from Saragossa, as his father hated all those soused hidalgos, those Marranos, as much as if they were devils;[32] instead, he had a fine wooden sword, and a dagger of boiled leather, painted and gilded in a way that would have pleased anyone.

His purse was made out of an elephant's bollock, which Herr Pracontal, Proconsul of Libya, gave him.[33]

For his robe they used 9,600 ells, less two-thirds, of blue velvet, as above, with gold tinsel threaded diagonally through it. The result was that if you looked at it from the right angle, an indescribable colour shimmered on it, like that you see on the necks of turtledoves. It was truly wonderful, and greatly delighted the eyes of those who saw it.

For his hat they used 302 ells and one-quarter of white velvet, and it was shaped broad and round to fit his head. His father said that those Arab Marrano bonnets, shaped like a pie crust, would one day bring misfortune to the shaven pates of their wearers.

For his plume, he wore a beautiful big blue feather taken from a pelican from the wild country of Hyrcania, daintily trailing over his right ear.

For the brooch on his hat he had a plate of gold weighing sixty-eight marks, bearing an emblem in enamel – the portrait of a human body with two heads facing each other, four arms, four feet and two arses, of the kind described by Plato in his *Symposium* as having been the form of human nature at its mystical beginnings. And around it there was written in Ionic characters:

ΑΓΑΠΗ ΟΥ ΖΗΤΕΙ ΤΑ ΕΑΥΤΗΣ[34]

To wear round his neck, he had a gold chain weighing 25,063 golden marks, made in the shape of great bayberries, between which there were set great green jaspers, engraved and cut into dragons all surrounded by rays and sparks, of the kind once worn by King Nekhepso[35]. And it hung down as far as the sphincter of his upper stomach. And all life long he derived benefit from it, as Greek doctors well know.

For his clothes, they used sixteen goblin skins and three werewolf skins to embroider them. And they were made of this material so as to follow the precepts of the Cabbalists of Saint-Louand.[36]

For his rings (which his father wished him to wear so as to renew the ancient insignia of nobility), he had on the index finger of his left hand a carbuncle as big as an ostrich egg, set in gold of Serapis, most elegantly. On the medical finger of the same hand, he wore a ring made of four metals set side by side in the most marvellous way you've ever seen, without the steel blending into the gold, or the silver overpowering the copper. The whole piece was made by Captain Chappuis, and Alcofribas, his fine assistant.[37] On the medical finger of the right hand he wore a ring made in spiral shape, on which were set a perfect balas ruby, a pointed diamond and a Physon emerald, all quite priceless. Hans Carvel, the great jeweller of the King of Melinda, assessed their value at 69,894,018 long-woolled sheep. The Fuggers of Augsburg gave the same value.[38]

CHAPTER 9
Gargantua's colours and livery

Gargantua's colours were blue and white, as you have read above. By these colours, his father wanted people to understand that this was a heavenly joy to him, white signifying joy, pleasure, delight and merriment, and blue, the things of heaven.

I can well understand that, as you read these words, you're having a laugh at an old boozer like me, as *you* think that this way of explaining the colours is perfectly criminal and quite abhorrent – for you, white means faith, and blue firmness. But without getting agitated, irritated, het up, or upset (it's not the weather for that), answer this question, if you don't mind. I'll not force you or use any constraint of any kind. I'll just tell you what I think, straight from the bottle's mouth.

So who's bugging you? Who's hassling you? Who's told you that white means faith and blue firmness? A silly little book that's sold by pedlars and booksellers under the title *The Blason of Colours*.[39] Who wrote it? Whoever it was, he showed enough caution not to put his name to it. As far as everything else goes, I don't know what I should most marvel at in him – his arrogance or his stupidity. His arrogance, which, without reason, without cause and without any likelihood, has dared to prescribe, on his own private authority, the meanings that would be denoted by colours: and this is how tyrants behave, believing that their mere say-so can be sufficient reason; it's not the way of the wise and the learned, who openly discuss their reasons and thus satisfy their readers. His stupidity, which has deemed that without any further demonstrations and valid arguments, everyone would allow his ridiculous rules to dictate their heraldic devices.

In fact (as the proverb says: in the arse of a man with the squitters, there's always plenty of crap), he managed to find a few idiots left over from the time of the high hats who have put faith in his work.[40] And they have tailored their apophthegms and sayings in accordance with it; they have harnessed their mules by it, dressed their pages, opened their breeches, bordered their gloves, put a fringe on their beds, painted their signs, composed songs and (what's worse) perpetrated impostures and cowardly tricks on the quiet, against public matrons.

In similar darkness are included those boastful fellows at court, always changing their names, who, wishing to use their heraldic devices to signify 'hope', depict a hoop; window panes for 'pains'; a melon and a cauliflower for 'melancholy'; the waxing moon with its two horns for 'a life of plenty'; a broken stone for 'stony broke'; a monk's soiled gown for 'a bad habit'; or a single man with a paintbrush for 'a bachelor of arts'.[41] But all these homonyms are so silly, so tasteless, so provincial and barbarous, that from now on, anyone who wants to use them in France, now that good literature has been restored, should have a foxtail attached to his collar and a mask of cow's turd plastered over his face. For the same reasons (if you can call them reasons, and not idle fancies), I would have a needle painted to denote that I am 'in need'. And a pepper pot, to show that my jolly roger can always 'pep up her pot'. And a row of urinals is a 'penal colony'. And a picture of an arsehole means 'full of good sense'. And my codpiece is 'that which passeth all understanding'. And my lady friend having a tinkle on her potty is 'chamber music'.

Quite different was the procedure of the wise men of Egypt in times gone by, when they wrote in letters that they called hieroglyphs. No one understood them who didn't understand the virtue, property and nature of the things that were figured by them, and everyone who did understand these latter things also understood the former. Orus Apollo has composed two books about them in Greek, and Polyphilius in the *Dream of Love* has gone into it in greater detail.[42] In France, you have a fragmentary version in the motto of My Lord the Admiral; it was first borne by Octavian Augustus.[43] But my little skiff will not venture any further amid these uninviting gulfs and shallows. I'm returning to put in at the port from which I set out. I do hope to write at greater length about all this one day, and show, both by philosophical reasons and by authorities accepted and approved ever since antiquity, how many colours there are in nature, and of what kind; and what may be signified by each colour, if God keeps my hatstand in shape, that old winepot of a headpiece – as my grandmother used to say!

CHAPTER 10
What is signified by the colours white and blue

So, white signifies joy, solace and gladness; and not without reason, but with every right and proper entitlement. You'll be able to verify this if you put your preconceptions behind you and are willing to hear what I'm going to tell you right now.

Aristotle says that, supposing you have two things that are of opposite species – good and evil, virtue and vice, heat and cold, white and black, pleasure and pain, joy and sorrow, and so on – if you couple them in such way that one opposite of one species goes reasonably well with the opposite of another, it follows that the other opposite will go well with the one that's left. For example: virtues and vice are opposite in one species; so are good and evil. If one of the opposites of the first species goes well with one of the second – like virtue and good (for virtue is necessarily good) – so will the two qualities that are left, namely bad and vice, since vice is bad.

Once you've grasped this logical law, take these two opposites, joy and sadness; then these two, white and black: they are physically opposite. So it is that black signifies grief, and so white will therefore quite justifiably mean joy. And this meaning was not laid down by human imposition, but accepted by universal consent – what the philosophers call *jus gentium*, universal law, valid in all countries. As you know pretty well, all peoples, all nations (I except the ancient Syracusans and a few Argives, who had twisted souls) and all languages, when wishing to make a public demonstration of their sadness, wear black clothes; and all grief is shown by black. This universal consent does not come about without nature providing some argument and reason in its favour; and anyone can understand it immediately without needing any further instruction from anyone else – this is what we call natural law.

By white, following the same natural induction, everyone has always understood joy, gladness, solace, pleasure and delight. In former times, the Thracians and Cretans signed their fortunate and joyful dates with white stones; and the sad and unhappy dates with black stones. Isn't night gloomy, sad and melancholy? It is black and dark by privation.

Doesn't brightness cheer the whole of nature? It is whiter than anything else. To prove this, I could refer you to the book Lorenzo Valla wrote against Bartolus,[44] but the witness of the Gospel will be enough for you. In Matthew, Chapter 17, it is said that at the transfiguration of Our Lord, *vestimenta ejus facta sunt alba sicut lux*, his raiment was white as the light. This shining whiteness signified to his three Apostles the idea and the nature of the joys of heaven, as all human beings are cheered by brightness. You have it on the word of an old woman without a tooth in her head: *Bona lux*, she said.[45] And Tobit, Chapter 5, when he had lost his sight and Raphael greeted him, replied, 'What joy could I have, who do not see the light of heaven?'[46] In this colour did the angels testify to the joy of the whole universe at the resurrection of the Saviour (John, XX), and at his ascension (Acts, I). In similar raiment did St John the Evangelist (Revelation, IV, VII) see the faithful clad in the heavenly and blessed Jerusalem. Read the old histories, both Greek and Roman, and you'll find that the town of Alba (the first model of Rome) was both built and named for the discovery of a white sow.[47] You'll find that, if anyone had won a victory over the enemy so that it was decreed he should enter Rome in triumphant state, he entered it on a chariot drawn by white horses. So did the man who entered it in ovation. No sign or colour could more effectively express the joy of their coming than white. You'll find that Pericles, Duke of the Athenians, decided that those of his soldiers who had drawn white beans by lot should spend the whole day in joy, solace and rest; the others, meanwhile, should fight in battle. There are a thousand other examples and instances that I could cite on this topic, but this is not the place.

Thanks to this information, you can solve a problem which Alexander of Aphrodisias considered insoluble: why does the lion, who merely with his loud roar terrifies all animals, fear and revere a white cock? The reason is (according to Proclus[48], in *De sacrificio et magia*, or *Sacrifice and Magic*) that the presence of the virtue of the Sun, which is the organ and storehouse of all earthly and heavenly light, is better symbolised by and related to the white cock than it is to the lion, both for its colour and for its specific order and property. Moreover, devils have often been seen in the shape of a lion, but in the presence of a white cock they immediately vanished. This is why the *Galli* (the Gauls or French, so called because they're naturally as white as milk, which the Greeks called *gala*) like wearing white plumes on their hats, being merry, open, gracious and likeable by nature; and for their symbol and emblem they have the flower that is whiter than all others, the lily.

If you want to know how by the colour white nature intends us to think of joy and gladness, my answer is that the analogy and similarity are as follows. As white externally decomposes and disperses the sight, clearly dissolving the optic spirits, in the opinion of Aristotle in his *Problems*, and that of the specialists in perspective (as when you travel across snow-covered mountains and complain that you can't see very well, as Xenophon writes happened to his men, and as Galen explains in more detail in Book 10 of *De usu partium*, or *The Use of Parts*), just as the heart, when affected by overwhelming joy, is inwardly dispersed and suffers from an evident dissolution of the vital spirits, so, when the joy is too excessive, it would be deprived of its sustenance, and hence life would be extinguished by this *pericharia* or surfeit of joy, as Galen says in Book 12 of *Method*, Book 5 of *De locis affectis*, or *Affected Areas*, and Book 2 of *De symptomaton causis*, or *The Causes of Symptoms*. That this happened in the past is attested by Cicero in Book 1 of the *Questio. Tuscul.*, or *Tusculan Disputations*, by Verrius, Aristotle, Livy (referring to the Battle of Cannae), Pliny, Book 7, Chapters 32 and 53, Aulus Gellius, Books 3 and 15, etc.; it happened to Diagoras of Rhodes, Chilon, Sophocles, Dionysius Tyrant of Sicily, Philippides, Philemon, Polycrata, Philistion, M. Juventus and others, who all died of joy. And as Avicenna says in his *Canon*, Book 2, and in *De viribus cordis*, or *The Strength of the Heart*, the same is true of saffron, which so cheers the heart that it robs it of life if it is taken in too big a dose, since it causes dissolution and excessive dilation.[49]

I've gone into this subject in rather more detail than I'd been planning to at the start. So at this point I'll strike my sails, leaving the rest to the book that will deal with it all in full. And, in a word, I'll simply say that blue certainly means heaven and heavenly things, in the same symbolic way that white signifies joy and pleasure.

CHAPTER 11
Gargantua's childhood

Gargantua, from the age of three to five years old, was brought up and educated in every suitable discipline as his father ordered, and he spent this time like other small children in his country, in other words, drinking, eating and sleeping; eating, sleeping and drinking; sleeping, drinking and eating. He was forever rolling around in the mud, getting a dirty nose and a mucky face. He wore out his shoes, often gaped after flies, and loved chasing flutterbies, over whom his father ruled. He pissed on his shoes, shat in his shirt, wiped his nose on his sleeves, and let his snot drip into his soup.[50] And he hung around all over the place, and drank out of his slipper, and made a habit of rubbing his stomach with a basket. He sharpened his teeth with a clog, washed his hands in his soup, and combed his hair with a goblet. He fell between two stools, flat on his bottom. He covered himself with a wet sack. He drank while he was eating his soup. He ate his cake without bread. He bit when he laughed. He laughed when he bit. He often spat into the basin, farted for fat, and pissed against the sun. He took shelter from the rain by standing in water. He struck while the iron was cold. He was empty-headed. He simpered. He puked his guts out everywhere. He jabbered his paternoster like a monkey. He kept coming back to the point. He took the water to horse. He blamed the dog for what the lion had done. He put the cart before the horse. He scratched where he didn't have an itch. He pulled the worms from his nose. He bit off more than he could chew. He ate his white bread first. He shod the grasshoppers. He tickled himself to make himself laugh. He ate like a pig. He made an offering of straw men to the gods. He had the Magnificat sung at matins, and thought it sounded most appropriate. He ate cabbage and shat leeks. He could spot flies in milk. He split hairs. He scraped the paper smooth. He soiled the parchment. He took to his heels. He swigged from the goatskin. He reckoned without his host. He beat about the bush and didn't catch a single bird. He thought that clouds were brass saucepans, and that bladders were lanterns. He killed two birds with one stone. He played the ass to get some bran. He made his fist into a mallet. He caught cranes at the first leap. He wanted coats of mail to be put together link by link. He always looked a gift-horse in the mouth. He told cock-and-bull stories about shaggy dogs. He put one ripe one between two that were still green. He made a ditch of the earth. He kept the moon from the wolves. If the clouds lowered, he hoped to catch skylarks. He made a virtue of necessity. He buttered his bread and lay on it. He cared as little about the shaven as about the clipped. Every day he puked his guts out (again). His father's little dogs ate out of his dish. He ate with them. He bit their ears, they scratched his nose. He blew up their arses, they licked his chops. And d'ya wanna know what, you guys? Here's to your hangovers! Well, darn me if that little drunkard wasn't always feeling up his nurses from top to toe and from up front to right behind – gee up, horsey! And he was already starting to exercise his codpiece. One day, his nurses decorated it with lovely bouquets of flowers, pretty ribbons, fine blooms, gorgeous bunches; and they spent their time pulling and rolling it between their hands, in the same way a pharmacist makes a suppository of ointment. Then they fell about laughing when it started to prick up its ears, as if they were really enjoying the game.

The one called it 'my little spigot', another 'my prick', another 'my coral branch', another 'my stopper, my cork, my gimlet, my ramrod, my drill, my pendant, my lusty frolicsome rollicking duster, my erector, my little red sausage, my tongue-tied little tailpiece'.

'It's mine!' one would say.

'It's mine!' would say the other.

'What about me?' would say a third. 'Don't *I* get anything? In that case, I swear I'm going to cut it off.'

'What, cut it?' said the other. 'That would be the most unkindest cut of all, madam. Do you cut children's thingies off? He'd be Mr Tail-less.'

And so that he could play like the small children in the region, they made him a lovely winch from the vanes of a Mirebeau windmill.

Then, so that he would be a good rider (especially of horses) all his life long, they made him a lovely big wooden horse, which he made to prance, jump, canter, charge and dance all at once, as well as walk, pace, trot, gallop, amble and go at the pace of a hobby, a hackney, a camel and an onager. And he made it change the colour of its hair, as monks change their chasubles, depending on feast days: bay, sorrel, dapple grey, rat colour, roan, cow, speckled, skewbald, piebald, white. And he himself, using a big beam set on wheels, made himself a hunting horse, and another one from the beam of a winepress for everyday use, and from a great oak a mule with a horse-cloth for his bedroom. And he had ten or twelve more for relays, and seven to act as post horses. And he had them all sleep next to him.

One day the Lord of Breadinbag visited his father, in great pomp and circumstance, the very same day as the Duke of Freeloader and the Count of Hotair. You can take my word for it, the accommodation was a bit cramped for so many people, especially the stables. So the chief steward and furrier of the aforementioned Lord of Breadinbag, enquiring whether there were any vacant stables available in the household, slipped over to Gargantua, still a young lad at the time, and quietly asked him where the stables for the big horses were, since they thought that children are happy to give away any kind of secret. So he led them up the great stairs of the château, crossing the second hall into a great gallery, via which they entered a great tower; and as they climbed up by different stairs, the furrier said to the chief steward, 'This kid is having us on: the stables are *never* in the upper storeys of the house.'

'That's just where you're wrong,' said the chief steward. 'I know places – at Lyons, La Baumette, Chinon and others too – where the stables *are* at the top of the house, so maybe there's an exit to the top storey at the back.[51] But I'll ask, so as to make sure.'

Then he asked Gargantua, 'Where are you taking us, my little chap?'

'To the stable,' he replied, 'where my big horses are. We'll soon be there – just have to climb up these stairs.'

Then, leading them across another great hall, he took them into his room and, opening the door, said, 'Here are the stables you were asking for. Here's my jennet, my gelding, my courser and my fine trotter. And handing over a great big lever to them, he said, 'I'm going to give you this Frieslander, which I got from Frankfurt. But he's all yours. He's a nice little horsey, very hard-working. With a goshawk tercel, half a dozen spaniels and two greyhounds, you'll be king of the partridges and hares all this winter.'

'By St John!' they said, 'we walked straight into this one! He's made a real monkey out of us.'

'Not at all,' he said. 'He's been here less than three days.'

Can you guess what they felt most like doing? Hiding themselves for shame, or laughing at the way they'd been taken in? As they were sheepishly making their way downstairs, he asked, 'Would you like an obblyonker?'

'What's that?' they asked.

'Five turds,' he replied, 'to make a muzzle for yourselves.'

'We've had quite enough for one day, thank you,' said the steward. 'We may be roasted, but we'll not catch fire in the flames – we've been greased all over, it strikes me. You little scamp, you've really taken the wind out of our sails; I can see you being pope one of these days.'

'That's just what I hope,' said Gargantua. 'But then you'll be a flutterby, and this fine popinjay will be a perfect hypocrite.'

'Maybe, maybe,' said the furrier.

'But,' said Gargantua, 'guess how many stitches there are in my mother's blouse.'

'Sixteen,' said the furrier.

'That's hardly gospel truth,' said Gargantua. 'There's a century's worth at the front, and a scent factory at the back, and you miscounted.'

'When?' said the furrier.

'When they made your nose into a spigot to make a hogshead of shit, and your throat into a funnel to pour into another vessel, as the bottoms had been blown out.'

'Blimey,' said the chief steward, 'this one's certainly got the gift of the gab. Master Chatterbox, I hope God preserves you from harm, your witty repartee is quite amazing.'

Anyway, as they were quickly making their way down the winding staircase, they dropped the big lever that he'd handed over to them. At which Gargantua said, 'Devil take it, you're dreadful bad horse riders, your curtal has left you quite curtailed. If you had to get to Cahusac, what would you prefer, to ride astraddle on a gosling, or lead a sow on a leash?'

'I'd rather have a drink,' said the furrier.

With these words, they came out into the lower hall, where the whole brigade had gathered. And when they recounted this latest adventure, they made everyone present laugh like a swarm of flies.

CHAPTER 13

How Grandgousier realised Gargantua's marvellous intelligence from his invention of an arse-wipe

Towards the end of Gargantua's fifth year, Grandgousier, returning from his defeat of the Canarians, came to pay his son a visit. There he was delighted, as any such father might be on seeing any such son. And he kissed him and cuddled him, and put all sorts of childish questions to him of every kind. And he drank deep with him and his nurses; and he took good care to ask them, among other similar things, if they had managed to keep him nice and clean. Gargantua replied that he had so arranged matters that throughout the whole land there was no boy cleaner than himself.

'How's that?' asked Grandgousier.

'I have,' replied Gargantua, 'by long and intensive experiments invented a means of wiping my arse which is the most lordly, the most excellent, the most efficient that has ever been seen.'

'What is it?' said Grandgousier.

'I'll tell you this minute,' said Gargantua. 'I began by wiping myself with the velvet mask of one of your ladies, and I found it was very comfy – the softness of the silk gave me great pleasure in my fundament. Another time, I used one of their hoods, and it was just as good. Another time, with a neckerchief, another time with ear-flaps of crimson satin; but the gilding on all the shitty little round bits in it scratched my whole bottom. May St Anthony's fire burn the bumgut of the goldsmith who made them, and that of the lady who wore them! I assuaged the pain by wiping myself with a page's bonnet which had a nice feather in it, Swiss-style. Then, while having a crap behind a bush, I found a March-born cat. I wiped myself with this, but its claws ulcerated my whole perineum. I cured myself of this the next day by wiping myself with my mother's gloves, well perfumed with fanny. Then I wiped myself with sage, fennel, anise, marjoram, roses, gourd leaves, cabbages, beets, vine leaves, mallows, mullein (which is as red as an arsehole), lettuce leaves and spinach leaves. All of this did my leg a power of good. Then I wiped myself with dog's mercury, persicaria, nettles and comfrey; but they gave me the bloody flux of Lombardy. I cured myself of this by wiping myself with my codpiece. Then I wiped myself with the bed linen, the blanket, the curtains, a cushion, a carpet, a green rug, a piece of rag, a napkin, a handkerchief and a dressing gown. In all of these I found more pleasure than people with a skin complaint do when they are given a vigorous rub-down.'

'That's all very well,' said Grandgousier, 'but which arse-wipe did you find best?'

'I was just coming to that,' said Gargantua, 'and you'll soon have the *tu autem* or *go in peace*. I wiped myself with hay, straw, rushes, litter, wool and paper. But:

> *You'll smear your balls if you use loo paper:*
> *It's better to find a different wiper.*

'What's all this?' said Grandgousier. 'My little bollocky boy, have you picked up the rhyming bug? You've got it from drinking, no doubt.'

'I certainly have,' replied Gargantua, 'my lord the king, I'm rhyming away already; and as I rhyme those words with these, I often start to cough and sneeze. Listen, this is what our loo says to those who are having a crap:

> *Shitty*
> *Squitty*
> *Farty*

Crapper,
What a whopper
Plopped on us!
Sloppy
Slimy
Stinky
Slithery,
May St Anthony's fire burn your arse
Unless
Your mess
You wipe
From every hole before you leave us!

'Do you want to hear any more?'
   'I certainly do!' said Grandgousier.
   So Gargantua said:

   '*I had a shit the other day*
   And realised how much I owe
   To my dear arse, in every way
   The smell was worse than that I know.
   If only someone without more ado
   Could've brought my gal to share my pooh
   While shitting.

   '*I'd have opened up wide her wee hole below*
   And shoved in my rain wand without any fear
   While she with her fingers refused to allow
   The shit to befoul my own dear rear
   While shitting.

'*Now* tell me I'm talking through my arse! By our Lady Muck, I didn't actually write that myself. But hearing old grandma here reciting it, I stored it away in the game bag of my memory.'
   'Let's get back to the main issue,' said Grandgousier.
   'You mean shitting?' said Gargantua.

'No,' said Grandgousier, 'arse-wiping.'

'Tell you what,' said Gargantua, 'will you pay me a puncheon of Breton wine if I make you look a fool?'

'You're on,' said Grandgousier.

'There's absolutely no need,' said Gargantua, 'to wipe your arse, unless you've done a pooh. There won't be any pooh unless you've had a shit. So we must shit before we can wipe our arses.'

'Ah, what a sensible little lad you are!' said Grandgousier. 'In days to come, as soon as I can, I'm going to have you made a doctor in gay science, by God I am. You are wiser than your years. So carry on with this arse-wiping discourse, please. And by my beard, for one puncheon you'll have sixty casks – of *good* Breton wine, I mean, which doesn't grow in Brittany, but in the fine land of Verron.'

'Afterwards, I wiped myself,' continued Gargantua, 'with a headscarf, a pillow, a slipper, a game bag and a basket. But, ouch! that arse-wiper was a real pain in the bum! Then with a hat. Note that when it comes to hats, some are flat, some furry, others velvety, others taffeta, and others satin. The best of all is the furry one, which is very effective at absterging the faecal matter. Then I wiped myself with a hen, a cock, a chicken, the hide of a calf, with a hare, a pigeon, a cormorant, a lawyer's bag, a hood, a coif and a lure. But in conclusion, I claim and maintain that there's no arse-wipe like a gosling with a nice covering of down, so long as you hold its head between your legs. Believe me, word of honour, you feel in your arsehole a quite mirifical voluptuousness, thanks both to the softness of that down and to the temperate warmth of the gosling, which is easily transmitted to the back passage and other intestines, eventually reaching the region of the heart and the brain. And don't imagine that the beatitude of the heroes and demigods who dwell in the Elysian fields has anything to do with their asphodel or their ambrosia and nectar, as these old women claim. It's due, in my opinion, to the fact that they wipe their arses with a gosling. And this is the opinion of Master Duns Scotus, too.

When he heard these things, the good Grandgousier was rapt with admiration, as he considered the lofty intelligence and marvellous discernment of his son, Gargantua. And he said to his nurses, 'Philip, King of Macedon, recognised his son Alexander's good sense at the way he could so dextrously handle a horse – the horse was so wild and unbridled that no one dared mount him, since he threw off all his riders, breaking the neck of one, the legs of another, the skull of another and the jawbones of another. As Alexander watched the horse in the hippodrome (this was the place where they put the horses through their paces and got them to perform their various tricks), he noticed that the reason the horse was behaving in such an unruly fashion was merely because he was scared of his own shadow. So, climbing onto him, he made him run into the sun, so that his shadow fell behind him, and by this means he made the horse docile to his will. Thereupon, his father realised what divine wisdom there was in him, and had him very well taught by Aristotle, who was at the time more highly esteemed than all the other philosophers of Greece.

'But let me tell you that merely from the talk I've just had with my son, Gargantua, in your presence, I realise that his understanding partakes of some divinity – I can see how very acute, subtle, profound and lucid it is. And he will reach the highest degree of wisdom, if he is well educated. For this reason, I intend to hand him over to some learned man to educate him as well as he can be educated. And I will spare nothing in doing so.'

So they placed him with a great and learned sophist called Master Tubal Holofernes, who taught him his alphabet so thoroughly that he could say it off by heart, backwards; this took him five years and three months. Then he read to him the *Donatus*, the *Facetus*, the *Theodolet*, and Alan of Lille's *In Parabolis*, or *Parables*; this took him thirteen years, six months and two weeks.[52]

But note that, in the meantime, he was teaching him to write in Gothic letters, and he wrote out all his books longhand, since the art of printing was not yet in use. And he habitually carried around a huge writing desk weighing more than seven thousand hundredweight. The pen case on it was as big and huge as the great pillars of Ainay; and the inkwell hung from it by great iron chains that were capable of bearing a ton of merchandise.

Then he read him the *De modis significandi*, or *Modes of Signifying*, with the commentaries of Windbreaker, Scoundrel, Blahblah, Galahad, John the Calf, Daft Ha'p'orth, Cunningus Linguisticus and a heap of others, and he spent more than eighteen years and eleven months over it. And he knew it so well that when he was given an exam, he could regurgitate it all by heart, backwards. And he could prove on his fingers to his mother that *de modis significandi non erat scientia.*[53]

Then he read him the *Compost*,[54] which he spent a good sixteen years and two months over, before his tutor passed away, and this was in the year 1420; he was laid low by the pox.

After that, he had another old wheezer named Master Jobelin Bridé, who read to him Hugutio, Hebrard's *Grecismus*, the *Doctrinal*, the *Pars*, or *Parts of Speech*, the *Quid est*, or *What Is…*, the *Supplementum*, Marmotret's *De moribus in mensa servandis*, or *A Guide to Table Manners*, Seneca's *De quatuor virtutibus cardinalibus*, or *The Four Cardinal Virtues*, *Passavantus cum commento*, and *Dormi secure*, or *Sleep Soundly*,[55] on high days and holidays. And a few others of the same kind. Reading these, he became as wise as any man we ever baked in an oven.

CHAPTER 15
How Gargantua was given other teachers

From all this, his father clearly saw that he really was studying very well and devoting all his time to it, and yet he wasn't deriving any benefit from it at all; and, what's worse, he was turning into an utter nincompoop, a half-soaked dozy so-and-so, and a total imbecile.

He complained about this to Don Philippe des Marais, Viceroy of Papeligoss, who told him that it would be better for his son to learn nothing at all rather than study such books with such teachers.[56] Their knowledge was mere stupidity and their wisdom a load of old rubbish which ruined all good, noble minds and corrupted the flower of their youth.

'I'll prove it,' he said. 'Take one of the young men of the present age – anyone who's studied for just two years; if he doesn't have better judgement, and greater eloquence and articulacy than your son, and isn't more at ease and capable of making a good impression in society, then consider me no better than a bacon-trimmer from the Brenne.' These words pleased Grandgousier, and he ordered that the suggestion be put into effect.

That evening at dinner, the aforesaid des Marais brought in a young page of his from Villegongys named Eudemon[57], so neatly combed, so spruced up, so well brushed and with such dignity in his bearing that he looked more like a little cherub than a man. Then he said to Grandgousier, 'You see this young lad? He's not twelve yet. If you don't mind, let's just see what a difference there is between the knowledge of your dopey daydreaming mataiologians[58] of bygone days and the young folks of today.'

Grandgousier was happy to try out the experiment and ordered the page to announce the topic of the debate. Then Eudemon, having first asked for the permission of the Viceroy, his master, took his stand, cap in hand, with an open face, a red glow on his lips and assurance in his eyes, with his gaze firmly fixed on Gargantua, a picture of youthful modesty; and began to praise and glorify him, firstly for his virtue and good behaviour, secondly for his knowledge, thirdly for his nobility, fourthly for his bodily handsomeness. And fifthly, he gently admonished him to revere his father in every observance, who was taking such pains to give him a decent education, and finally begged him to condescend to take him on as the least of his servants. At present, there was no gift that he desired from heaven, other than being granted the favour of having an opportunity to please him by performing some agreeable service. And the page uttered all these words with such appropriate gestures, such clear pronunciation, such an eloquent voice, and such ornate and perfectly Latinate language that he seemed more like a Gracchus, a Cicero or an Aemilius of bygone days than a stripling of our own age.

But the best Gargantua could do in reply was to start crying like a cow, and to hide his face in his cap. And they couldn't get a single word out of him, any more than you can get a fart out of a dead donkey. At this, his father was so enraged that he wanted to kill Master Jobelin. But the aforesaid des Marais held him back, dissuading him so eloquently that his wrath was diminished. So he ordered that Jobelin be paid his wages and given a nice sophistical leaving party with plenty of booze; and then he could go to hell. 'At least,' said Grandgousier, 'he won't cost his host much, if – here's hoping – he dies as drunk as an Englishman.'

When Master Jobelin had left the house, Grandgousier consulted with the Viceroy as to which tutor they could give his son; and between the two of them it was decided that they would give the position to Ponocrates[59], Eudemon's tutor, and that they'd all head off to Paris, to find out how young men of France studied at that time.

CHAPTER 16
How Gargantua was sent to Paris on the back of an enormous mare, and how she overcame the ox flies of the Beauce region

In this same season, Fayolles, the fourth king of Numidia,[60] sent from Africa to Grandgousier the most huge and enormous mare that had ever been seen, and the most monstrous too. As you know perfectly well, there's always something new out of Africa. This mare was as big as six elephants, and had its feet divided into toes, like Julius Caesar's horse, its ears hanging like the nanny-goats of Languegoth[61], and sported a little horn in her arse. Apart from that, she had a coat of burnt sorrel, dappled all over in grey. But above all, she had a horrible great tail. Give or take a little, it was as huge as the Saint-Mars pillar near Langeais; and, like the pillar, it was square, with its tufts just as tightly woven as ears of wheat.

If you're amazed at this, you should be even more amazed at the tails of Scythian rams, which weighed more than thirty pounds, and those of Syrian sheep. If you can believe Thenaud, people had to hitch a wagon to their rumps to carry those tails, they were so long and heavy.[62] Now you can't say the same about *your* tails, you old lechers from the lowlands.

And this mare was brought across by sea in three carracks and a brigantine, as far as the port of Olonne in the Talmont region. When Grandgousier saw it, he said, 'This is just what we need to carry my son to Paris. Hoppla! Now, by God, everything's going to be all right. He's going to be a cleric one of these days! If it weren't for my lords the beasts, we'd all live like clerics.'

The following day, after a drink or three (as you can well imagine), they set off: Gargantua, his tutor Ponocrates, and his retinue, together with Eudemon, the young page. And because the weather was fair and quite mild, his father had some tawny boots made for him. Babin calls them buskins.[63]

And so they merrily rode along, enjoying every minute of the journey, until they came to a place not far from Orléans. Here there was a huge forest, thirty-five leagues long and seventeen or so leagues wide. It was filled with the most dense and horrid swarm of ox flies and hornets, so that it was a real brigands' lair as far as the poor mares, donkeys and horses were concerned. But Gargantua's mare took justified vengeance on all the outrages perpetrated in this forest on the animals of its own species, by playing a trick on the insects that they'd never even suspected. As soon as the party had entered the aforesaid forest and the hornets had launched their assault, she unsheathed her tail and, flicking it this way and that, swatted them all away so effectively that she flattened the whole wood, swatting without rhyme or reason, up and down, hither and thither, to and fro, above and below, flattening the wood in the same way a reaper cuts down grass. As a result, there hasn't been a wood there ever since, nor any hornets. The whole country was reduced to open fields. When Gargantua saw this, he was delighted, though he realised it was none of his doing. And he told his servants, 'I like this country, though I can't *boast* that I made it look like this.' Ever since, this region has been called the *Beauce* – but all they had for lunch was a yawn. And in memory of this, even these days, the gentlemen of the Beauce still lunch on yawns, and feel very well for it, and spit all the better.

Finally, they arrived in Paris. Here, Gargantua relaxed for two or three days, living it up with his friends, and enquiring what knowledgeable men there were in town just then, and what people's favourite tipple was.

CHAPTER 17

How Gargantua paid his welcome to the Parisians;
and how he took the great bells of Notre-Dame

A few days after, when they'd rested enough, he visited the city; and he himself was a star attraction. The people of Paris, after all, are such stupid, idle gawpers, and so idiotic by nature, that a juggler, a pedlar of indulgences, a mule with its jangling bells or a fiddler at the crossroads, will get a bigger gathering than a good evangelical preacher would. And they crowded round him and hassled him so much that he was forced to sit down for a rest on the towers of the church of Notre-Dame. As he sat there and surveyed all the people gathered round him, he said in a loud, clear voice, 'I think these rascals want me to pay them my welcome and my *proficiat*.[64] Fair enough. I'll give them their wine. But only as a joke: *oui! oui!*'

Then, with a smile, he undid his fine codpiece, and, pulling his willy out, wee-wee'd over them so ferociously that he drowned 260,418 of them, besides women and children. A few of them managed to escape this flood of piss by taking to their heels. And when they'd got to the top of the hill where the University stands, sweating, coughing, spitting and all out of breath, they started to swear and blaspheme, some of them out of anger but others with Parisian gaiety, 'Carymary, carymara, Holy Mum, what a thing! This isn't what we meant by *Paris in the spring*!' Hence the origin of the expression. Formerly, Paris had been called Leucecia, as Strabo says (Book 4), i.e. 'Little White Lady' in Greek, because the ladies who live there have such white thighs.[65] And also, as they were giving their city its new name, the Parisians all swore by the saints of their parishes; these Parishians are a motley crew, and naturally good swearers, including of oaths, and therefore good jurists, and a bit inclined to having too high an opinion of themselves. That's why Joaninus de Barranco, in his *De copiositate reverentiarum*, or *An Encyclopedia of Polite Turns of Phrase*, claims that the Greek name for them is 'Parrhesians', i.e. 'haughty in speech'.[66]

After this Gargantua gazed at the great bells that were in the aforesaid towers and made them chime really harmoniously. As he did so, the thought occurred to him that they would be just perfect as jingles to hang round the neck of his mare, which he wanted to send back to his father heavily laden with cheeses from Brie and fresh herrings. And so he took them back to his lodging.

However, a Commander of Hams of the Order of St Anthony came along begging for hog meat:[67] wanting to make himself heard at a distance, and make the bacon quake in people's larders, he tried to make off with the bells on the quiet. But – decent chap as he was – he left them there, not because they were too hot to handle, but because they were just a bit too heavy to carry. (He wasn't the fellow from Bourg, who's a personal friend of mine.)

The whole city was in noise and uproar – as you know, they start rioting so easily that foreign countries are amazed at the patience of the kings of France, who use no unjust force to keep them in order, even though they cause a real nuisance day after day. I wish to God I knew in which workplace these schisms and plots are forged, so I could point them out to the confraternities of my parish!

As you can well believe, the place where the people gathered, hopping mad and quite beside themselves, was Nesle, where at that time (it's since disappeared) was the oracle of Lutetia.[68] There the complaint was set out, and the inconvenience of the purloined bells was asserted. After they had spent time arguing *pro* and *con* and *thus* and *therefore*, it was concluded *in baralipton*[69] that they'd send the oldest and most expert member of the Faculty to Gargantua to point out the horrible inconvenience the loss of these bells represented for them. And notwithstanding the criticisms of some members of the University, who claimed that this was more of a job for an orator than for a sophist, the man elected to carry out the assignment was the most reverend Master Janotus de Bragmardo.[70]

CHAPTER 18
How Janotus de Bragmardo was sent to recover the great bells from Gargantua

Master Janotus, with a Caesarean haircut, wearing his theological lyripipion[71], and with his stomach well antidoted with baked quinces and holy water from the cellar, took himself over to Gargantua's lodgings, driving before him three beadles with red schnozzles, and dragging along behind him five or six Masters of Artlessness, who'd all given themselves a good wash and were thus all perfectly filthy.[72]

At the entrance, Ponocrates met them. He had to suppress a movement of alarm when he saw them all in fancy clothes, and thought they must be some crazy mummers. Then he enquired of one member of that gang of artless masters what this mummery could mean. The answer was that they were asking for the bells to be returned to them.

As soon as he had heard this, Ponocrates went to tell Gargantua, so he could be ready with an answer, and decide without delay what should be done. Gargantua, informed of the events, called to one side Ponocrates, his tutor, Philotimon[73], his steward, Gymnast, his squire, and Eudemon, and conferred with them briefly about what should be said and done. They were all of the opinion that the visitors should be taken to the buttery and there made to drink like country lads, and so that the old wheezer wouldn't get too big-headed about the bells being returned at *his* request, they should, while he was busy having a few drinks, send for the city provost, the dean of the Faculty, and the church priest, to whom they would hand back the bells even before the sophist had announced the object of his mission. After this, in the presence of all these people, they'd hear his fine harangue.

This was all done, and when the above-mentioned people had arrived, the sophist was brought into the main hall and began as follows, coughing and spluttering.

CHAPTER 19

*The harangue of Master Janotus de Bragmardo to Gargantua,
asking him to return the bells*

'Ahem, ahem, hem. *Mna dies*, sir, *mna dies*. *Et vobis*, gentlemen.[74] It would only be fair for you to let us have our bells back. We really need them, you see. Ahem, ahem, harrumph! Not long ago we turned down good money for them, offered by people from London in Cahors, as well as from Bordeaux in Brie – they wanted to buy them for the quasimodal quality of the elementary complexion that is enthronified in the terresterility of their quidditative nature to extraneise the fogs and fierce storms on our vineyards, not ours, I mean, but right nearby.[75] If we lose our plonk, we lose everything, we lose our heads and our whole way of life.

'If you agree to my request and return them, I'll have earned myself six strings of sausages and a lovely pair of trousers; they'll be just the thing for my legs unless they turn out to belie their promise. Ah, by God, *domine*, there's nothing like a pair of trousers! *Et vir sapiens non abhorrebit eam*.[76] Aha! Not everyone's got a pair of trousers; I know as much from personal experience. I think you ought to know, *domine*, I've been metagrobolising[77] this fine harangue for eighteen days. *Reddite quae sunt Caesaris, Caesari, et quae sunt Dei, Deo. Ibi jacet lepus*.[78] Take my word for it, *domine*, if you want to have dinner with me, *in camera*, by Jiminy *charitatis, nos faciemus bonum cherubin. Ego occidi unum porcum et ego habet bonus vina*.[79] You can't get the Latin wrong if the wine's right! So let's be having you, *de parte Dei, date nobis dingallingas nostras*.[80] Look, I'll give you, on behalf of the Faculty, a Sermones de Utino, *que, utinam*, you'll give us our bells back.[81] *Vultis etiam pardonos? Per diem, vos habebitis et nihil payabitis*.[82] O Sir *domine, dingallingadonnaminor nobis. Dea, est bonum urbis*.[83] Everyone uses them. If your mare likes having them, so does our Faculty, *que comparata est jumentis insipientibus, et similis facta est eis, psalmo, nescio quo*; yup, I'd jotted it down in my notepad, *et est unum bonum Achilles*.[84] Ahem, ahem, harrumph! Look, I'll prove that you should give them back to me. *Ego sic argumentor: omnis dingalinga dinga-lingabilis in dingalingerio dingalingando dingalingans, dingalingativo*

47

dingalingare facit dingalingabiliter dingalingantes. Parisius habet dingalingas. Ergo gluc![85] Ha, ha, ha! That's telling 'em! It's in *tertio primi*, in *Darii*, or somewhere or other.[86] Upon my soul, the time has been when I was a real devil in argument. But these days I just go rabbiting on. And all I need now is some good wine, a comfy bed, my back to the fire and my belly to the table, and a nice deep bowl. Ah, *domine*, I beg you, *in nomine patris et filii et spiritus sancti, Amen*,[87] give us back our bells, and God keep you from harm, and our Lady of Health, *qui vivit et regnat per omnia saecula saeculorum, Amen*.[88]

'Ahem, ahahem, ahahahem, ahahahahahem! *Verumenim vero, quando quidem, dubio procul, edepol, quoniam, ita certe, meus deus fidus*,[89] a city without bells is like a blind man without a stick, a donkey without a crupper, and a cow without cowbells. Until you've given them back to us, we won't stop crying after you like a blind man who's lost his stick, braying like a donkey without its crupper, and bellowing like a cow without cowbells.

'A certain Latinist who lives near the Hôtel-Dieu once said, on the authority of one Tapponus, no, I'm wrong, it was Pontanus, a secular poet,[90] that he wanted them to be of feathers, with the clapper made out of a foxtail, since they gave him an attack of chronic in the tripes of his brainpan when he was composing his carminiform poems. But anyway, with a hey and a dee and a hey-diddle-dee, biff! baff! he was declared a heretic. They're like putty in our fingers. I rest my case. *Valete et plaudite. Calepinus recensui.*'[91]

CHAPTER 20
How the sophist took home his cloth;
and how he took his learned colleagues to court

No sooner had the sophist finished than Ponocrates and Eudemon burst out laughing, so heartily that they thought they were going to give up the ghost, just like Crassus when he saw a bollocky donkey eating thistles, and Philemon, who, when he saw a donkey eating the figs prepared for dinner, died of laughter.[92] And Master Janotus joined in with them, so that each of them was laughing more than the others, so much that tears came to their eyes by the vehement concussion of the substance of the brain; whereupon those lacrymal humidities were expressed, and forced to flow out along the optic nerves. And thereby they represented Democritus heraclitising, and Heraclitus democritising.[93]

When their laughter had quite subsided, Gargantua consulted with his companions as to what to do. Ponocrates voiced the opinion that they should give this great orator another drink. And seeing that he'd given them more fun, and made them laugh more than Daydreamer the Clown,[94] he should be given the ten strings of sausages mentioned in his merry harangue, with a pair of trousers, three hundred big logs of firewood, twenty-five hogsheads of wine, a bed with three layers of goosedown, and a strong, deep bowl, all of which he said were necessary for his old age.

All of this was done just as they had decided – except for the fact that Gargantua (doubting that they would easily find any suitable trousers for his legs, and also unsure as to which style would best suit the aforesaid orator: the martingale, which is a drawbridge at the backside so you can crap more comfortably, or the mariner's model, so as to relieve his kidneys more readily, or the Swiss variety, to keep his pot belly warm, or the kind with a codtail so as to prevent his loins getting overheated) had seven ells of black cloth delivered to him, and three ells of white wool for the lining. The wood was carried by the porters, the masters of arts carried the sausages and the bowl, Master Janotus himself wanted to carry the cloth. One of the aforesaid masters of arts, Jocko Stiffy, told him off, pointing out that this was neither decent nor proper for a man in his position, and that he ought to give it to someone else.

'Aha!' said Janotus, 'you complete ass, you're not drawing the right conclusion *in modo et figura*. That's what the *Suppositions* are for, and the *Parva logicalia. Panus pro quo supponit?*'[95]

'*Confuse*,' said Stiffy, 'and *distributive*.'[96]

'I'm not asking you, you ass, *quon supponit*, but *pro quo*,'[97] said Janotus. 'And the answer, you ass, is *pro tibiis meis*.[98] And for that reason I'll carry it *egomet, sicut suppositum portat adpositum*.'[99] And so he slipped off with it, just as Patelin ran off with his cloth.[100]

The best thing about it all was when the old wheezer vaingloriously claimed his trousers and sausages right in the middle of a session at the Mathurins[101]. They were immediately refused him, since he'd been given them by Gargantua, as was now common knowledge. He retorted that this had been Gargantua's free gift, an act of pure generosity, and in no way did it release them from *their* promises. Notwithstanding this, they replied that he should be content with the perfectly reasonable reward he'd been given, and not ask for a scrap more.

'Reasonable?' said Janotus. 'As if we were ever reasonable here! You lousy cheats, you worthless scum. You're the wickedest scoundrels that ever walked the face of the earth. I know how it goes: *don't limp in front of a lame man*. I've treated you maliciously, have I? By God's spleen, I'm going to tell the King about the dreadful, monstrous things that go on here, thanks to your meddlesome plotting and scheming! And I'll be a leper if he doesn't have you all burnt alive, as buggers, traitors, heretics and seducers, enemies of God and virtue!'

At these words, they drew up an indictment against him. He in turn had them issued with a summons. In short, the lawsuit was retained by the court, and it's still going strong. The masters vowed, on this point, that they would never wash again; Master Janotus and his supporters vowed in turn that they'd never wipe their noses, unless a definitive decision was reached. As a result of these vows they've stayed there ever since, all dirty and snotty, as the court has still not sifted through all the evidence. The verdict will be handed down at the next Greek Calends, viz., never. As you know, they go into quite *unnatural* detail, even scrutinising their own articles. Now the articles of Paris sing that God alone can do infinite things. Nature makes nothing immortal: she sets an end and term to all things that she has made. And *omnia orta cadunt*,[102] etc. But these swallowers of the morning fogs turn the lawsuits that are pending before them into things both infinite and immortal. By so doing, they have given rise to, and proven, the saying of Chilo the Lacedaemonian[103] consecrated at Delphi, namely that poverty and lawsuits go together, and those who bring lawsuits are made poor and wretched: they come to the end of their life sooner than they reach the end of their suit.

CHAPTER 21
Gargantua's studies, as set out by his sophistical tutors

So the first days went by, and the bells were put back in their place, and the citizens of Paris, to show their gratitude for Gargantua's decency, offered to look after and feed his mare for as long as he liked. Gargantua was glad to accept. And they sent her to live in the Forest of Bière.[104] I don't think she's there any more.

That done, he was very eager indeed to study as Ponocrates saw fit. But Ponocrates began by ordering him to behave in the same way as he was accustomed to, so he could find out how it was that for so long his former tutors had made him so empty-headed, foolish and ignorant.

So he arranged his time in such a way that ordinarily he woke between eight and nine o'clock, whether it was daylight or not. That was what his former governors had ordered, citing the words of David: *Vanum est vobis ante lucem surgere.*[105] Then he would frolic, roll and stretch out in bed for some time, so as to get his animal spirits nice and frisky, and he would put on whatever clothes best suited the season, but he was especially fond of wearing a great long robe of thick frieze, furred with fox skins. Then he would comb his hair with Herr Handy's patent comb, i.e. four fingers and one thumb – as his tutors had told him that it was a waste of his time on earth to comb, wash and clean himself in any other way. Then he went for a crap and a piss, threw up, burped, farted, yawned, spat, coughed, sobbed, sneezed and blew his nose like an archdeacon, and had breakfast to blow off the fogs and bad air: nice fried tripe, tasty carbonadoes, delicious hams, lovely grilled young goat and plenty of matins soup. Ponocrates told him off, pointing out that he shouldn't eat so soon after getting out of bed without having first taken some exercise, but Gargantua replied, 'What? Haven't I had quite enough exercise already? I rolled around six or seven times in bed before I got up. Isn't that enough? Pope Alexander did the same, on the advice of his good Jewish doctor, and he lived right up to his death, in spite of the envious. My first masters got me into the habit, saying that breakfast improved one's memory, and that was why they had their first drink then. I feel well on it, and dine all the better. And Master Tubal (who graduated top of his class when he took his first degree in Paris) told me that it's not going for an early jog that is so good for you, but rather setting out first thing; likewise, the entire health of our human frame doesn't consist in drinking gulp after gulp after gulp, like ducks, but rather in drinking the minute you're up. *Unde versus:*[106]

> '*Get up too soon and you'll feel all surly:*
> *Best have your first drink nice and early.*'

After a hearty breakfast, he went off to church, and his servants carried a huge breviary all bundled up in a big basket that weighed, if you include the grease as well as the clasps and parchment, more or less eleven hundredweight and six pounds. There he would hear twenty-six or thirty masses. Meanwhile the priest who had come to say his prayers for him would take up position, muffled like a hoopoe, with his breath all nicely antidoted with plenty of syrup of plonk. Gargantua accompanied him as he mumbled all these kyries, and told his beads so carefully that not a single one of them fell to the ground. On leaving the church, they brought to him, on an ox-cart, a great load of Saint-Claude rosaries, each of them as big as the round thing you put your hat on. And as he walked through the cloisters, galleries or garden, he would recite more of them than sixteen hermits.

Then he'd study for a brief half-hour or so, his eyes fixed on his book, but (as the comic writer puts it) his soul in the kitchen. Then, pissing a whole urinal full, he'd sit down to table. And as he was phlegmatic by nature, he would begin his meal with a few dozen hams, smoked oxtongues, botargoes, chitterlings and other such spurs to wine. Meanwhile, four of his servants would throw into his mouth, one after the other, without stopping, whole shovelfuls of mustard. Then he'd take a horrific great swig of white wine, to relieve his kidneys. After that he would eat, depending on the season, meat to suit his appetite, and he stopped eating as soon as his belly was starting to hang down. As for drinking, he never stopped, but drank without rhyme or reason – he said that the limits and bounds of drinking were when, as a person drank, the cork on his slippers swelled upwards a good half foot.

CHAPTER 22
Gargantua's games

Then, mumbling and chumbling his way through a slice of after-dinner grace, he would wash his hands with fresh wine, pick his teeth with a pig's trotter, and have a nice little natter with his chums. Then, when the green cloth was laid out, they'd bring out plenty of cards, dice and a supply of game boards.

There he would play at:

Flush,[107]
Primiera,
Grand slam,
Robber,
Trumps,
Prick and spare not,
One hundred,
The spinet,
Old maid,
Cheat,
Ten-and-pass,
Trente-et-un,
Pair and sequence,
Three hundred,
Beggar my neighbour,
Odd man out,
Turn the card,
Poor Jack,
Lansquenet,
Cuckold,
Next man speak,
Teetotum,
Marriage,
Got it,
Opinion,
Follow-my-leader,

Sequences,
Cockall,
Tarots,
Loser wins,
Snap,
Torture,
Snorer,
Rummy,
Honours,
Morra,
Chess,
Fox and geese,
The men's morris,
Pick-a-back,
Raffles,
Speculation,
Three dice,
Knucklebones,
Nick-nock,
Lurch,
Queen's game,
Sbaraglino,
Backgammon,
Poker,
All fall down,
Dogsbody,
Needs must,
Draughts,
Mop and mow,
Primus, secundus,
Scrabble,
Go,
Whist,
Odds or evens,
Heads or tails,
Knuckle-bones,

Spillikins,
Lawn billiards,
Hunt the slipper,
The moping owl,
Shooting the bunny,
Tug of war,
Piggy-in-the-middle,
Mick, Nick and the Maggies,
The horn,
The Shrovetide ox,
Two little dicky birds,
Keep a straight face,
Pinpricks,
Call my bluff,
Sheep to market,
Horsey,
I sit down,
Shit-in-his-beard,
Buskins,
Pin the tail on the donkey,
Chucker-out,
Pass the parcel,
It,
Out he goes,
Cocking snooks,
The fly,
Darts,
Throw-it-up,
Tobogganing,
Hold the pass,
Selling oats,
Blow the coal,
Hide and seek,
Hopscotch,
Irons out of the fire,
The crusty clown,

Nine-stones,
Piggy-back,
The finding of the saint,
Hinch-pinch,
Pear tree,
Bumbasting,
The Breton jig,
Oats and beans,
The sow,
Belly to belly,
Cubes,
Pushpin,
Quoits,
The ball is mine,
Fouquet,
Nine-pins,
The return course,
Skimming,
The dart,
A-roaming-we-will-go,
Skipping,
Sly Jack,
Short bowls,
Shuttlecock,
Dogs' ears,
Smash the crockery,
My desire,
Whirligig,
Rush bundles,
Short staff,
Blind beggar,
Spur away,
Sweepstakes,
The ferret,
The pursuit,
Peanuts,

In a row,
The cherry pit,
The humming-top,
The whip-top,
The peg-top,
The hobgoblin,
Scarred face,
Pushball,
Fast and loose,
Fatarse,
Ride a cock-horse,
Saints alive,
The brown beetle,
Lions and tigers,
Fair and gay goes Lent away,
The forked oak,
Leap-frog,
What's the time, Mr Wolf,
Fart-in-throat,
Nuts in May,
The swing,
The shock of wheat,
Noughts and crosses,
Baste the bear,
Tic-tac-toe,
Twenty questions,
Nine hands,
Just a minute,
The fallen bridges,
Hangman,
Bull's-eye,
Battledore and shuttlecock,
Blindman's bluff,
Bob-cherry,
Spy,
Froggit,

Cricket,
Pestle and mortar,
Cup and ball,
The queens,
Tinker, tailor,
Heads and points,
Dot to dot,
Wicked death,
Marbles,
Lady, I wash your cap,
The bolting cloth,
Wild oats,
Greedyguts,
Windmills,
Help!,
Pirouetting,
Seesaw,
Hind the ploughman,
Sliding,
The witch's hat,
The dead beast,
Climb the ladder,
The dead pig,
The salt rump,
The bird has flown,
Twos and threes,
Nearly there,
Jump in the bush,
Crossing,
No skipping,
Which hand?,
I can't go on,
Heads or tails?,
Don't give up,
Gunshot crack,
Mustard-pounder,

Truant,
The relapse,
The feathered dart,
Duck your head,
Bull's-eye,
Keep going,
Slash and cut,
Bang on the nose,
What a lark,
Flicks.

After they had played well, and sifted, strained and bolted the time, they decided to have a little drink, i.e. eleven southern-style gallons per man, and straight afterwards they banqueted and then, on a comfy bench or in a nice big bed, they stretched out and took a nap for two or three hours, without an evil thought in their heads or an evil word on their lips.

When Gargantua woke up, he waggled his ears a bit. Meanwhile, some fresh wine was brought over, whereupon he drank better than ever. Ponocrates pointed out to him that it was not good for him to drink like that straight after sleeping. 'But,' replied Gargantua, 'it's exactly the same way the holy fathers live. My nature is such that as I sleep I get all salty, and sleeping has the same effect on me as ham.'

Then he started to study a bit, and paternoster away; to get shot of his prayers more quickly, he'd climb onto an old mule which had served nine kings. And so, his lips mumbling and his head nodding, he would set off to pick up a rabbit or two that had got caught in the snares.

On his return, he made his way to the kitchen to find out what roast was on the spit. And he'd have a very good dinner, you can take my word for it! – he especially liked inviting over some of his neighbours, those who were good drinkers, and as they all matched each other drink for drink, they would tell all sorts of stories old and new. Among others, his domestics included the lords du Fou, de Gourville, de Grignault and de Marigny.

After dinner, the nice wooden gospels would appear – a supply of gameboards, in other words, or a nice game of flush, one, two, three, or a game of 'chance' to make it short. Or else they would go to see the local wenches, and enjoy midnight feasts, with snacks and more snacks. Then he slept continuously until the next day at eight o'clock.

CHAPTER 23
How Gargantua was taught by Ponocrates in such a disciplined way that he did not waste a single hour of the day

When Ponocrates saw how disordered Gargantua's way of life was, he determined to adopt a quite different method to teach him literature; but for the first days he put up with his earlier habits, knowing that nature will not endure sudden changes without great violence.

And so as to make a more efficient start to the task in hand, he asked a learned physician of the time, Master Theodore by name, to see if he could not set Gargantua back on a better track. Theodore purged him canonically[108] with hellebore of Anticyra and, by means of this medicine, cleaned out all the products of the deterioration and perverse habits his brain had fallen into. By this same means, Ponocrates also made him forget all that he had learnt under his former tutors, in the same way that Timotheus used to do with his pupils who had been taught by other musicians.[109]

To perform this task more effectively, he introduced him to the companies of learned people who were there, in emulation of whom there grew up in him a spirited impulse and desire to study in a different way and acquire a reputation for himself. After, he set him to study so hard that he didn't waste a single hour of the day, but consumed all his time in literature and honourable learning.

So, Gargantua now woke at about four in the morning. As they were giving him a rub-down, there was read out to him a page of the holy scriptures, loud and clear, with a suitable care for correct pronunciation. To this task they assigned a young page from Basché, Anagnostes by name.[110] Following the main points and themes of this lesson, Gargantua would frequently abandon himself to reverence, adoration, prayer and supplication of the good Lord, whose majesty and marvellous judgement were amply demonstrated by the reading.

Then he would go to the privy place to make an excretion of his natural .digestions. There his tutor would repeat what he had read, going over the more obscure and difficult points.

As they returned, they would consider the state of the sky, whether it was the same as they had noted the evening before; and what signs the sun, as well as the moon, was entering on that day. Then he was dressed, his hair was combed, he was tidied, accoutred and perfumed, during which time they repeated the lessons of the previous day to him. He himself recited them by heart; and he would apply them to several practical cases and extend them to the human condition as a whole – sometimes this went on for two or three hours, but usually it ended when he was completely dressed. Then for three solid hours they read to him.

After this, they would venture out of doors, still discussing the topic of the lesson; and they would have a game in the Bracque,[111] or in the fields, and play ball, or tennis, catching in threes, giving their bodies plenty of good, vigorous exercise, just as they had previously exercised their souls. They were quite free and unconstrained in their play, leaving off the game when they felt like it – they usually broke off when their bodies started to sweat or when they were in any other way tired. So, when they had been well dried and rubbed down, they changed their shirts and, strolling along unhurriedly, they went to see if dinner was ready. As they waited, they recited, clearly and eloquently, some of the expressions remembered from the lesson.

Meanwhile, Sir Appetite came knocking at the door, and when the time came, they sat down to table. At the start of the meal, they read out to Gargantua some entertaining story of derring-do from days gone by, until he'd taken his wine. Then (if they felt like it) they continued with the reading, or started up a lively and enjoyable discussion – talking, during the first months, about the virtue, property, efficacy and nature of everything that was served to them at table: the bread, the wine, the water, the salt, the meats, the fish, the fruits, the herbs, the roots, and how to prepare them. As they did so, he rapidly learnt all the relevant passages in Pliny, Athenaeus, Dioscorides, Julius Pollux, Galen, Porphyry, Opian, Polybus, Heliodorus, Aristotle, Aelian and others. During these discussions, they would often have these books brought to table so they could check they had got their facts right. And he learnt the things they said so thoroughly and remembered them so accurately that there wasn't a physician of the time who knew half the things he did. After that, they talked over the lessons that had been read that morning, and they finished their meal with a confection of quince, while he picked his teeth with a mastic toothpick, washed his hands and eyes with cool fresh water, and gave thanks to God with a few fine canticles composed in praise of his munificence and divine loving kindness.

After this, they had cards brought over, not for a game, but to learn a thousand nice little tricks and new inventions from them. These all had to do with arithmetic. In this way, he developed a liking for this science of numbers, and every day, after dinner and supper, he would spend his time as pleasantly as he had previously done playing dice or cards. He learnt so much arithmetic this way, both in theory and in practice, that Tunstal the Englishman, who had written a great deal about it, confessed that really, in comparison to Gargantua, he himself understood it no better than he did High German.[112] And Gargantua also learnt not only this but also the other mathematical sciences, such as geometry, astronomy and music. As he waited for the coction and digestion of his meal, they made up a thousand merry little geometrical figures and instruments, and at the same time they applied the laws of astronomy. Afterwards, they relaxed by singing musical songs in four and five parts, or else on a set theme, to their throats' content. As regards instruments of music, he learnt to play the lute, the spinet, the harp, the German flute and the nine-holed flute, the viol and the sackbut.

Having put this hour to good use and digested his food, he purged himself of his natural excrements. Then he settled down again to his principal topic of study for three hours or more – both repeating that morning's reading and continuing with the book they had started, as well as writing and learning how to draw and form the ancient Roman letters.

After this, they left their lodgings, taking with them a young gentleman of Touraine, the squire Gymnast, who showed Gargantua the art of chivalry. And so, after changing his clothes, he would climb onto a courser, a jennet, an Arabian or a light horse, and give him a hundred laps, making him pirouette in the air, jump the ditch or the gate, and trot round in a circle, going both to the left and to the right. He didn't break a lance – it's the emptiest boast in the world to say, 'I broke ten lances in the tourney', or 'in battle'; a carpenter could do it just as easily. But what *is* highly praiseworthy is with a single lance to have broken ten of one's enemies. So, with his sharp-pointed steel lance, all stiff and strong, he would break open a door, transfix a harness, uproot a tree, spit a ring, carry off an armed saddle, a hauberk and a gauntlet. All this he did armed cap-à-pie.

As for making his horse keep time to the blare of the trumpets, and making little clicks with his tongue to encourage him, nobody did it better than he did. The horse jumper from Ferrara was a mere ape in comparison.[113] In particular, Gargantua was a real expert in leaping quickly from one horse to another without touching the ground (these horses were called 'desultory'[114]), as well as in mounting from either side with lance in hand, without stirrups, and guiding the horse where he wanted to without a bridle. Such things are useful for military discipline.

Another day he would exercise with a battleaxe. He could wield it so well, pulling it back so strongly from every thrust, and lowering it so supplely in order to lash out in a circle, that he would have passed as a knight-at-arms on campaign and in all trials. Then he would brandish the pike, swing the two-handed sword, the hack sword, the Spanish rapier, the dagger and the poniard, both armed and unarmed, with a buckler, a cape or a small round shield.

He would go hunting the stag, the roebuck, the bear, the fallow deer, the boar, the hare, the partridge, the pheasant, the bustard. He played big ball, and made it bounce up into the air, either kicking it or punching it. He wrestled, ran, jumped – though not with a hop, skip and a jump, nor with the German jump (Gymnast said that such jumps are useless and no good in war). But with one bound he would leap over a ditch, fly over a hedge, run six paces up a wall, and in this way climb up to a window that was one lance-length high. He would swim in deep water, rightways up, on his back, on his side, with his whole body, just with his feet, one hand in the air, and, holding a book aloft, he would cross the whole River Seine without getting it wet, and trailing his coat along in his teeth, as did Julius Caesar. Then with one hand he would haul himself into the boat, and then throw himself back in the water, head first, sounding the depths, exploring the hollows of the rocks, plunging deep down into the abysses and gulfs. Then he would turn the boat, steering it whichever way he wished, swiftly, slowly, with the current, against the current, holding it fast in the sluice, steering it with one hand and with the other using a great oar to practise his fencing with. He would hoist the sail, climb the mast by the shrouds, run along the rigging, adjust the compass, lower the bowlines, and hold the rudder firm. When he finally strode, completely refreshed, from the water, he would go on to climb the mountain, and come down just as easily. He climbed trees like a cat, jumped from one to another like a squirrel, and knocked down great branches, as if he had been another Milo[115]. With two sharp steel daggers, and two tried and tested stabbers he would climb to the top of a house like a rat, and then come down again with such lightness of limb that he wasn't the slightest hurt by the fall.

He could put the stone, throw the dart, the javelin, the boar-spear and the halberd; he could draw the bow, bend the strong siege cross-bow, aim the harquebus with the naked eye, set the cannon on its mounting, shoot at the mark, at the popinjay target, uphill, downhill, in front, to the side and to the rear like the Parthians. They would tie a cable for him to some high tower, so that it hung down to the ground; he'd climb up this with both hands, then slither down it so quickly and so safely that you couldn't have equalled it even on a level plain. They set up a great pole for him between two trees; he would hang from it by both hands, and swing to and fro on it, without his feet touching anything at all – you'd never have caught up with him even running at top speed.

And to exercise his thorax and lungs, he would shout out like all the devils. I once heard him calling Eudemon, who was in Montmartre, from the Saint-Victor Gate. Stentor didn't have such a powerful voice at the Trojan War. And in order to stiffen up his sinews, they'd made two great weights of lead, each of which weighed 8,700 quintals, which he called his dumbbells. He would lift them up in each hand, and raise them into the air over his head, and hold them in that position without moving for three-quarters of an hour or more, so matchless was his strength.

He could play prisoner's base with the best of them. And when the time for the scrum came, he would stand so sturdily on his feet that he could let the most daring of them try to budge him from his place, as Milo did in bygone days. And in imitation of Milo he would also hold a pomegranate in his hand and give it to anyone who could manage to wrest it from him.

Having thus spent his time, he was rubbed down and cleaned, and given a change of clothes, and then he would saunter back, passing through some meadows, or other grassy places, and examine the trees and plants, comparing them with the books of ancient writers who mention them, such as Theophrastus, Dioscorides, Marinus, Pliny, Nicander, Macer and Galen,[116] and he would take great armfuls of them back to his lodgings, where he entrusted them to a young page, Rhizotome[117] by name, who also looked after the mattocks, pickaxes, grubbing forks, spades, pruning knives and other instruments necessary for good botanising.

When they had arrived at their lodgings, while supper was being prepared, they would repeat some passages from what had been read and sit down at table. Note at this point that his dinner had been sober and frugal – he simply ate just enough to keep the worms from biting; but his supper was copious and generous. He took exactly as much as he needed to keep himself going and nourish himself. This is a *real* diet as prescribed by the art of good, reliable medics – even if any number of crap doctors, overworked and harassed in the surgeries of the sophists, advise the contrary.

During this meal, the reading from supper was continued, for as long as seemed right. The rest of the time was taken up in pleasant conversation, good literary talk – all very useful. When they had given thanks for their meal, they occupied themselves with music (singing and playing harmonious instruments), or little pastimes like the games and tricks you play with cards, dice and goblets. And there they would remain, enjoying themselves to the full, and sometimes making merry until it was time for sleep. Sometimes they would go off to pay a visit to men of letters, or people who had been in foreign parts.

When night had completely fallen, before they retired to bed, they would go to the place in their lodgings from where they had the clearest view of the sky, and there note the comets – if there were any about – and the figures, situations, aspects, oppositions and conjunctions of the stars.

Then with his tutor he would briefly go over all that he had read, seen, learnt and heard in the course of the entire day, just as the Pythagoreans used to do. Then they would pray to God the Creator, adoring him and proclaiming their faith in him, and glorifying him for his immense goodness, and giving him thanks for all the time past, and commending themselves to his divine mercy for the entire future. Whereupon, they would go off to enjoy their repose.

CHAPTER 24
How Gargantua spent the time when the weather was rainy

If the weather happened to be rainy and intemperate, the whole period preceding dinner was spent in the usual way, except that he had a nice bright fire lit to make up for the inclemency of the weather. But after dinner, instead of taking physical exercise, they would stay at home and, by way of healthy activity, they would have fun baling hay, splitting and sawing wood, and threshing the wheatsheaves in the barn. Then they would study the art of painting and sculpture; or they would bring back the ancient game of knucklebones, as Leonicus has described it, and as our good friend Lascaris plays it.[118] As they played, they would go over the passages in ancient authors where there is mention of such games, or some metaphor based on them; likewise they would go to see how metals were drawn, or artillery cast; or they would go to visit the lapidaries, goldsmiths and cutters of precious stones, or the alchemists and coiners, or the makers of great tapestries, the weavers, the velvet-makers, watchmakers, mirror-makers, printers, organ-makers, dyers and other such kinds of workmen, and they would hand out gratuities on all sides, as they learnt and examined the industry and inventive skills of different professions. They would go to hear public lectures, solemn acts, rehearsals and declamations, the pleadings of gentle lawyers and the harangues of evangelical preachers. Gargantua would pass through the halls and places appointed for fencing, and there, against past masters, he would try his hand with every kind of weapon, and show them all clearly that he knew as much if not more about it than they did. And instead of botanising, they would visit the druggists' shops, the herbalists and the apothecaries, and carefully examine the fruits, roots, leaves, gums, seeds, exotic unguents, and all the ways they were adulterated. He would go to see the jugglers, conjurors and quacks hawking around their panaceas; and he would pay great attention to their gestures, their ruses, their legerdemain and their skilful patter, especially those from Chauny in Picardy, since they are by nature great gabbers and grand tellers of tall tales about green monkeys.

When they had come back for supper, they ate more soberly than on other days, and drier and less fattening foods, so that the dampness and inclemency of the weather, communicated to the body by inevitable proximity, would thereby be corrected, and they would not be incommoded by not having taken any physical exercise, as they usually did.

This was the education given to Gargantua, and so he went on from day to day, benefiting as much from it as you can well imagine in a young man of his age, endowed with good sense and able to sustain the pace; though it seemed difficult to begin with, as he persevered, it came to seem so gentle, easy and delightful that it seemed more like a king's pastime than a schoolboy's studies. However, Ponocrates, to give him some respite from the intense concentration of his mind, advised him once a month, on some nice, clear, settled day, to head out with his friends, leaving town in the morning for Gentilly, or Boulogne, or Montrouge, or the Charenton Bridge, or Vanves, or Saint-Cloud. And there they would spend the entire day really enjoying themselves to the best of their abilities, joking with each other, jesting, matching each other drink for drink, playing, singing, dancing, rolling around in some lovely meadow, robbing sparrows' nests, catching quails and fishing for frogs and crayfish. But even though this day was spent without books and readings, it was not spent without profit. In their lovely meadow, they would recite by heart some delightful poetry – Virgil's *Georgics*, Hesiod, the *Rusticus* of Poliziano – and they would quote a few charming epigrams in Latin, then turn them into rondeaux and ballads in French. As they banqueted, they would separate the water out from diluted wine (as Cato teaches in his *De re rustica*, or *Agriculture* and Pliny too), with a goblet of ivy, washing the wine in a basin full of water, then drawing it out with a funnel, pouring the water from one glass to another, and building several little automata, i.e. machines that move themselves.[119]

CHAPTER 25
How the cake-makers of Lerné and those from Gargantua's country fell to quarrelling, which led to mighty wars

At this time, which was the harvesting season, at the beginning of autumn, the local shepherds were guarding the vines and preventing the starlings from eating the grapes. And just then, the Lerné cake-makers were passing down the great highway, leading ten or twelve loads of griddle cakes to town.

The shepherds requested them most politely to give them some of those cakes in return for money, at the market price. It is, you see, quite heavenly to breakfast on grapes with fresh griddle cakes, especially Pinot grapes, fig grapes, muscadines, verjuice grapes and laxative grapes for those suffering from a constipated stomach – they make you do a big one, as long as a lance; and it often happens that people, thinking they are simply going to fart, actually shit themselves, whence the name of these grapes: 'harvesters' curse'.

The cake-makers weren't in the least bit inclined to grant their request – worse, they hurled insults at them, calling them beggars, snaggletooths, carrot-headed ninnies, a waste of space, shitabeds, stupid clowns, two-faced gits, lazy buggers, guzzlers, pot bellies, boasters, swaggerers, bumpkins, wierdoes, spongers, sabre-rattlers, idle little poseurs, apes, lazybones, fatheads, crazy fools, cretins, jokers, mutton dressed as lamb, miserable wretches, shitty herdsmen and other such defamatory epithets. And they added that there was no way *they* deserved to eat such nice cakes, but should think themselves happy to be able to eat coarse bread and round loaves.

In response to this hail of insults, one of them, Forgier by name, a thoroughly decent man by nature and a noteworthy young fellow, replied mildly, 'How long have *you* been so bullish, then? You've turned really thuggish. Good Lord, you used to be perfectly happy to give us some cakes, and now you're refusing? That's no way to treat good neighbours – *we* don't behave like that when you come here to buy our fine wheat to make all your cakes and pastries from. We'd have happily thrown in some of our grapes too, but, by Our Lady Muck! you might well live to regret this, and one day you'll be hearing from us. Then we'll pay you back as you deserve, don't you forget!'

Then Marquet, the main standard-bearer of the company of cake-makers, told him, 'D'you know something? You're pretty cocky this morning. You ate too much millet last night. Just you come over here, and I'll give you a piece of my cake…'

Then Forgier went over, in all innocence, taking an eleven-denier coin out of his baldric, thinking that Marquet was going to bring out some cakes for him. But the latter gave him such a heavy lash of his whip across his legs that the welts showed. Then he made as if to gallop off as fast as he could, but Forgier shouted, 'Help! Murder!' at the top of his voice, as loud as he could; and he hurled at Marquet a thick cudgel that he carried under his arm, which hit him on the coronal suture of his head, above the crotaphic artery, on the right side, with the result that Marquet fell off his mare, looking more dead than alive.

Meanwhile, the farmers, who were shelling walnuts nearby, came running up armed with their great poles and started thrashing those cake-makers for all they were worth. The rest of the shepherds and shepherdesses, hearing Forgier's shouts, came up with their slings and catapults, and let off a great volley of such small stones that they seemed like hail. Finally, they caught up with them, and relieved them of some four or five dozen of their cakes. Still, they *did* pay them the going price, and gave them a hundred walnuts and three basketfuls of white grapes. Then the cake-makers helped Marquet to remount – he was severely wounded – and made their way back to Lerné without continuing along the road to Parillé, uttering the direst threats to the herdsmen, shepherds and shepherdesses of Seuillé and Sinays.

Then the shepherds and shepherdesses had a real feast with those cakes and fine grapes, and had a good old laugh together, as they listened to the merry sound of the bagpipes; they made fun of those snooty cake-makers, who had more than met their match for not having crossed themselves with the correct hand that morning. And with plump chenin grapes they made a very neat poultice for Forgier's legs, so that his wound was soon healed.

CHAPTER 26
How the inhabitants of Lerné, at the command of their king, Picrochole, launched a surprise attack on Gargantua's shepherds [120]

The cake-makers returned to Lerné and immediately, even before having anything to eat or drink, made their way to the capitol, where, in front of their king, whose name was Picrochole, third of that name, [121] they set out their grievance, showing their baskets broken, their hats battered, their dress all torn, their cakes stolen away, and in particular Marquet's terrible wound; and they said this had all been done by Grandgousier's shepherds and farmers, near the great highway just beyond Seuillé.

He straight away flew into a towering rage, and without any further ado, not stopping to ask the whys or the wherefores, he had all of his subjects summoned throughout his territory, ordering each and every one of them, on pain of the gallows, to assemble in arms in the main square, in front of the château, at midday. So as to underline the seriousness of his enterprise, he sent his drummer to drum all around the town. He himself, while his dinner was being prepared, went off to have his artillery made ready, and his ensign and banner unfurled, and a supply of munitions loaded up – munitions for the belly as well as weapons to fight with.

At dinner, he handed out his commissions, and on his command, Lord Stingy was put in charge of the vanguard, which numbered 16,014 harquebusiers, and 35,011 soldiers of fortune. Principal squire Swashbuckler was put in charge of the artillery, which numbered 914 great bronze guns – cannons, double cannons, basilisks, serpentines, culverins, large and small, bombards, falcons, bases, and other pieces. The rearguard was under the command of Duke Pennypincher.

In the main body of the army were the King and the princes of his kingdom.

Rapidly armed and accoutred in this way, before setting out, they sent three hundred light horses, under the command of Captain Windswallower, to reconnoitre the land and find out whether there was any ambush waiting for them out in the fields. But after they had carefully searched everywhere, they found the whole surrounding countryside was peaceful and quiet, without any sort of gathering.

Hearing this, Picrochole ordered that each soldier should march under his banner, at speed. And so, without order or restraint they spread out across the fields, pell-mell, wasting and pillaging everywhere they went, without sparing either rich or poor, or any place sacred or profane. They made off with oxen, cows, bulls, calves, heifers, ewes, sheep, nanny-goats and billy-goats; hens, capons, chickens, goslings, ganders and geese; pigs, sows and piglets; they knocked down walnuts, harvested vines, carried off vinestocks, and shook down all the fruit from the trees. They left behind them an unprecedented trail of disorder. And they encountered nobody to resist them; everyone flung themselves on their mercy, begging for more humane treatment in view of the fact that they had at all times been good and friendly neighbours, and had never committed any excess or outrage against them that might have led to them being so suddenly assailed like this, and God would shortly punish them for it.

These pleas and threats were met with no reply except that *they would teach them to eat cake.*

CHAPTER 27
How a monk of Seuillé saved the abbey close from being sacked by the enemy

So they went on, wreaking havoc, pillaging and thieving, until they reached Seuillé, where they stripped the men and women of their belongings and took everything they could; there was nothing too hot or heavy for them. Although there was an epidemic of plague and it was present in the greater part of the houses, they entered everywhere and made off with everything inside – and yet at no time did any of them run any risk of catching it. And this is quite amazing. After all, the priests, curates, preachers, doctors, surgeons and apothecaries who had gone to visit, bandage, cure, preach to and admonish the sick had all died of the infection, and these pillaging, murdering devils suffered no ill effects whatsoever. How does that come about, gentlemen? Think about it, I implore you.

When they had pillaged the town, they made their way to the abbey making a horrid and tumultuous din, but they found it all locked up and closed. So the main part of the army marched on, towards the Ford of Vède, except for seven companies of foot soldiers and two hundred lances, who stayed put and broke down the walls of the close so as to ruin the whole vintage.

Those poor devils of monks didn't know which of their saints to turn to. In an attempt to outface all eventualities, they had the bells rung *ad capitulum capitulantes*.[122] There it was decreed they would form a fine procession, reinforced with some eloquent preachifying and litanies *contra hostium insidias*, and fine responses *pro pace*.[123]

In the abbey there was at that time a claustral monk named Brother John of the Mincemeat, young, ardent, frisky, cheerful, good with his hands, bold, adventurous, resolute, tall, thin, with a nice wide mouth and a splendid prominent nose, a fine dispatcher of hourly prayers, a fine dismantler of masses, a fine polisher off of vigils – in a word, a real monk if ever a monk there was since the monking world first monked in a monkery. Apart from that, a cleric to the marrow of his bones when it came to the breviary.

When he heard the noise the enemy was making throughout the close of their vineyard, he came out to see what they were up to. And seeing that they were harvesting the vineyard, which provided him and his comrades with drink for the whole year, he went back to the heart of the church where the other monks had gathered, as dazed as bell-founders, and saw that they were singing, '*Ini, nim, pe, ne, ne, ne, ne, ne, ne, tum, ne, num, num, ini, i, mi, i, mi, co, o, ne, no, o, o, ne, no, ne, no, no, no, rum, ne, num, num.*'[124]

'What use is this stupid sing-song?' he exclaimed. 'God Almighty, why don't you sing, "Farewell, baskets, your work's done, Harvest-time has come and gone"?' Devil take me if they're not in our close and cutting the vinestocks and grapes down so efficiently that for Chrissakes there'll be precious little gleanings to be had for the next four years! St James's belly! What are we poor devils going to drink meanwhile? Lord God, *da mihi potum*.'[125]

Then the claustral prior said, 'What's this old soak doing here? Off to prison with him! Disturbing the divine service like this!'

'But let's make sure, brudder,' replied the Monk, 'that we don't let *dee wine* service be disturbed – you yourself, Lordy Prior, enjoy a glass of dee best now... and so does any decent gent. A noble man is never averse to good wine. That's a monastic first principle. But this is no time for the responses that you're singing here, by God! Why are our breviary hours so short when it's the season for harvest and vintage, and so long during Advent and throughout winter? The late Friar Macé Pelosse[126] of happy memory, a true zealot of our religion (devil take me if I'm mistaken), told me, ah, I remember it well, that the reason was this: so that during the harvest season we would ensure the wine was well pressed and laid down, and then, in winter, drink it. Listen, gentlemen, all of you – anyone who loves wine should follow me, by God! St Anthony's fire burn me, I swear it, if anyone will get a drop of wine if they haven't come to the aid of the vine! God's belly – it's Church property we're talking about! No, I tell you, no! Devil take it, St Thomas of England was ready to die for Church property; if I were to die for the same reason, wouldn't I be a saint like him? But *I'm* not going to be the one to die – the others can do that for me.'

Saying this, he stripped off his great habit and seized his staff and cross, which was made from the heart of a sorb-apple tree, long as a lance, round in shape to fit in a fist, and decorated here and there with fleurs-de-lis, by now rather faded. And so he sallied forth in his fine cassock, with his frock slung scarfwise. And with his staff and cross he laid so vigorously into the enemy soldiers who, without order or banner, trumpet or drum, were harvesting throughout the close – the standard-bearers and ensigns had laid down their standards and ensigns at the foot of the walls, the drummers had smashed in one side of their drums so they could fill them with grapes, and the trumpets had been filled with whole bunches of them; everyone was on the rampage – so, he crashed into them so hard, without a single word of warning, that he bowled them over like pigs, lashing out right and left, in good old fencing style.

With some soldiers he dashed their brains out, with others he broke their arms and legs, with others he dislocated the vertebrae of their necks, with others he demolished their kidneys, knocked off their noses, blackened their eyes, split open their jaws, smashed their teeth down their throats, shattered their shoulder blades, flayed their shins, knocked their thighbones out of their sockets and pulverised their forearms. If anyone tried to hide among the thicker vinestocks, he would give him a good drubbing up and down the spine and a good thrashing round the loins, like a dog. If anyone tried to run away, he would dash his head into pieces with a blow to the lambdoidal suture. If any climbed up a tree, thinking they would be safe there, he took his stick and rammed it up their arses. If anyone he knew from a long while back called out, 'Ahoy there, Brother John, my old pal, Brother John, I surrender!' he would reply, 'Well, you don't have much choice! Surrender you shall – your soul to the devils.' And he'd give him a good beating. And if any were so infected by overweening boldness that they tried to stand and face him, he would demonstrate the strength of his muscles – transfixing them through the chest, piercing their mediastinum and heart. With others, he lunged at the hollow of their ribs and turned their stomach topsy-turvy, so that they promptly perished. With others, he struck so ferociously at their navels that he made their tripes come pouring out. With others he thrust right between the bollocks and pierced them through the bumgut. Take my word for it: it was the most horrible spectacle the world has ever seen.

Some of them started calling on St Barbe, others St George, others St Handsoff, others Our Lady of Cunault, Our Lady of Loretto, of Good News, of La Lenou, of Rivière. Some commended themselves to St James, others to the Holy Shroud of Chambéry – but it got burnt three months later, so thoroughly that they were unable to save a single shred of it; others prayed to Cadouin, others to St Jean d'Angely, others to St Eutropius of Saintes, to St Mesmes of Chinon, to St Martin of Candes, to St Clouaud of Sinays, to the relics of Javrezay, and a thousand other nice little saints.[127]

Some of them died without speaking, others spoke without dying. Some died as they spoke, others spoke as they died. Others cried out aloud, 'Confession! Confession! *Confiteor! Miserere! In manus!*'[128] So loud were the cries of the wounded that the prior of the abbey came out, accompanied by all his monks. And when they saw those poor folk knocked over amid the vines and mortally wounded, they gave confession to some of them. But while the priests were busy confessing them, the little monklets went running up to the place where Brother John was, and asked him how he wanted them to help him. He replied that they should slit the throats of those he had laid low. So, leaving their great capes on a trellis nearby, they started slitting throats and finishing off those he had already wounded. Do you know what weapons they used? Fine whittles, which are little half-knives that children in our part of the world use to shell walnuts.

Then, wielding his staff and cross, he reached the breach that the enemy had made. Some of the monklets carried off the ensigns and standards to their rooms, to make them into garters. But when those who had made their confession tried to get out through the same breach, the Monk beat them to a pulp, saying, 'This lot have confessed and repented, and obtained pardons. They'll go straight to Paradise – straight as a sickle blade, or the road to Faye!'[129] And thus by his valour were defeated all those of the army who had entered the close, a good 13,622 of them, without women and children – that goes without saying. Never did Maugis the Hermit bear himself so valiantly, using the length of his pilgrim's staff against the Saracens (of whom it is written in the epic *Tale of the Four Sons of Aymon*), as did the Monk against the enemy with his staff and cross.[130]

CHAPTER 28
How Picrochole took by storm La Roche Clermaud; and Grandgousier's compunctions and regrets about having to go to war

As the Monk was skirmishing, as we have said, against those who had entered the close, Picrochole in all haste passed over the Ford of Vède with his men and attacked La Roche Clermaud. Here he met with no resistance whatsoever, and because night had already fallen he decided to lodge with his soldiers in that town, and cool down his pungitive wrath.

The following morning, he carried by storm the bulwarks and the château, and fortified it strongly, and supplied it with the munitions necessary, thinking that he would be able to retreat here if he were attacked elsewhere, as the place was strong both by art and by nature, because of its position and site.

Anyway, let's leave them there and return to our good friend Gargantua, who is still in Paris, intent on the study of literature and athletics, and good old Grandgousier, his father, who, after supper, is warming his bollocks in front of a big, fine, blazing fire, waiting for the chestnuts to roast, and writing on the hearth with a stick burnt at one end, the kind you use to poke the fire with, as you tell your wife and family splendid stories from bygone days.

One of the shepherds who was guarding the vineyards, a man named Pete, came up to him just then and gave a full account of the excesses and pillages committed by Picrochole, King of Lerné, in his lands and domains, and how he had pillaged, wasted and sacked the whole area, except the close of Seuillé, which Brother John of the Mincemeat had saved, to his honour; and how at present the aforesaid king was at La Roche Clermaud, where in great haste he was fortifying himself, he and his men.

'Alas! Alas!' said Grandgousier, 'what's all this, my friends? Am I dreaming, or is what I've been told true? Picrochole, my old comrade (we go back for ever), my friend by race and alliance – coming here to attack me? Who has urged him to do so? Who spurs him forward? Who is leading him on? Who advised him to do such a thing? Oh, oh, oh, oh, oh! My God, my Saviour, help me, inspire me, advise me on what I should do. I protest, I swear before you, so may you show your favour to me, if I ever caused him any displeasure or harmed his people, or carried out any pillage in his lands… quite the contrary, I have helped him with men, money, favours and advice, in all cases where I could see it would be of help to him. For him to have committed such an outrage against me can only be the work of the evil spirit. My Lord, you know my mind, and nothing can be hidden from you. If by chance he has gone mad and you have sent him here so that I can restore his mind, give me both the power and the wisdom to return him to the yoke of your holy will by good discipline. Oh, oh, oh! Good people, my friends and trusty servants, am I going to have to call on you to help me? Alas! All I needed in my old age was rest and quiet, and all my life I have striven for nothing so much as peace. But I can see all too well that I ought now to load down my poor weak and feeble shoulders, and take my lance and mace into my trembling hand, to come to the aid and support of my poor subjects. Reason decrees it – after all, I am maintained by their labour and nourished by the sweat of their brow, I myself, and my children and my whole family. But in spite of all this, I will not undertake war until I have tried all the arts and means of peace. That is something I am resolved on.'

So he summoned his council and set out the situation just as it was. And it was concluded that they would send some man of sense and experience to Picrochole to find out why he had suddenly broken out of his state of peace and invaded lands to which he had absolutely no claim. Furthermore, they would send for Gargantua and his companions, so they could keep the country running and defend it, if need be. All of this pleased Grandgousier, and he commanded that it be done as agreed.

So he immediately sent his lackey, Basque, to seek out Gargantua with all speed. And he wrote to him as follows.

CHAPTER 29
The tenor of the letter Grandgousier wrote to Gargantua

The fervour of your studies would long have made me hesitate before bringing you back from that philosophical repose, were it not that the presumption of our friends and former confederates has now robbed my old age of its security. But since fateful destiny so decrees, and I am now troubled by those in whom I had placed most trust, I am forced to recall you to the aid of the people and property that are entrusted to you by natural law. Just as weapons are weak outside the home if good council is not within, likewise, vain is the study, and futile the council, which is not at the opportune moment put into practice and effect by virtue.

It is not my aim to provoke, but to appease; not to attack, but to defend; not to conquer, but to protect my loyal servants and hereditary lands. Into these has entered, with hostile intent, Picrochole, without cause or pretext, and from day to day he is pursuing his crazed and furious enterprise with excesses that are intolerable to free men. I have made it my duty to moderate his tyrannical wrath, offering to him all that I thought might satisfy him; and on several occasions I have sent to him in all friendship, to find out how, by whom and in what way he felt that he had been so insulted; but from him the sole reply I have had was one of wilful defiance, and the claim that he was merely taking over my lands, over which he had a natural right to rule. In this way I realised that the eternal God had abandoned him to the rudder of his own free will and his own designs – which can only ever be wicked, unless continually guided by divine grace; and that God, in order to confine him to his proper station and bring him back to his senses, had sent him here with hostile intent against me.

Therefore, my beloved son, as soon as you can, once you have read this letter, return in all haste to bring help, not so much to me (even though piety should naturally impel you to do so) as to your people, whom you can, by the use of your reason, succour and safeguard. This exploit is to be accomplished with the least bloodshed possible. And if there is any means of so doing, we will use more expedient devices, stratagems and ruses of war, to save all souls and send them back home rejoicing.

Dearest son, may the peace of Christ our Redeemer be with you. My greetings to Ponocrates, Gymnast and Eudemon. This 20th September.

Your father,

GRANDGOUSIER

CHAPTER 30
How Ulrich Gallet was sent to Picrochole

Once this letter had been dictated and signed, Grandgousier ordered that Ulrich Gallet, his master of requests, a wise and discreet man, whose virtue and good advice he had already tried and tested in various disputes and contentions, should go to Picrochole, to put forward their case as they had decreed.

Good old Gallet set off that very same hour and, having passed the ford, he asked the miller about Picrochole's position. The miller answered that his soldiers had left him neither rooster nor hen, and they had shut themselves up in La Roche Clermaud, and he advised him not to go any further, for fear of the watch – their crazed fury was quite overwhelming. Gallet could easily believe this, and for that night he lodged at the miller's.

The next morning, he made his way with the trumpeter to the gate of the château and requested the guards to let him speak to the King – it would be to his advantage to hear. When these words were announced to the King, he refused downright to open the gate to him, but came out onto the bulwarks and said to the ambassador, 'What's new? What have you got to say?' So the ambassador spoke as follows.

CHAPTER 31
The speech made by Gallet to Picrochole

'No more just cause for sorrow can arise between human beings than that, where they had a right to expect grace and benevolence, they should receive distress and injury. And not without cause (albeit without reason), several, finding themselves in such a dire situation, have felt this indignity to be more intolerable than the loss of their lives. And when they have been unable, either by force or by any other stratagem, to remedy the situation, they have deprived themselves of the light of life.

'It is thus no wonder if King Grandgousier, my master, is, at the sight of your furious and hostile arrival, filled with the greatest displeasure, and gravely troubled in spirit. It would be cause for amazement if he had not been affected by the unprecedented excesses that, on his lands and against his subjects, have been perpetrated by you and your soldiers, who have committed every conceivable example of inhumanity. This is, in itself, such a great grievance to him, given the heartfelt affection with which he has always cherished his subjects, that no mortal man could feel it more. However, it is even more grievous, indeed, beyond human reckoning to him, that it is by you and your men that these injuries and wrongs have been committed – you, who within memory, and from all antiquity, both you and your forefathers, had established a friendship with him and all his ancestors, a friendship which, until now, you had together kept inviolable, safeguarding and maintaining it as a sacred alliance, so much so that not only he and his people, but even the Barbarian nations (Poitevins, Bretons, Manceaux and those who live beyond the Canary Isles and Isabella), deemed that it would be as easy to demolish the firmament, and raise the deep abysses above the clouds, as to sever your alliance. And they so feared it, in all their undertakings, that they never dared to provoke, irritate or injure either of you, for fear of the other.

'There is more. That sacred friendship has so filled these climes that there are today few inhabitants of the whole continent and the Ocean islands who have not nursed the ambition to be received into it, on terms and pacts that you yourselves would determine. They reckoned your confederation to be as valuable as their own lands and domains. The result has been that, within memory, there has been no prince or league so crazed with pride and boldness as to try and invade, not just your lands, but even those of your confederates. And if by over-hasty council they did in fact attempt some sudden enterprise against them, the minute they heard the name and title of your alliance, they immediately abandoned their venture.

'So what fury impels you now – all alliances broken, all friendship trodden underfoot, all rights transgressed – to invade his lands with hostile intent, without having been in any way by him or his people injured, vexed or provoked? Where is faith? Where is law? Where is reason? Where is humanity? Where is the fear of God? Do you really think that these outrages are concealed from the eternal spirits and the sovereign God, who brings just retribution on our deeds? If you do think so, you are mistaken: all things will come before his judgement. Is it fateful destinies or the influence of the stars which are working to end your ease and repose? All things have their end and period. And when they have come to their highest pinnacle, they are thrown down in ruin; they cannot remain in that state for long. Such is the end of those who cannot by reason and temperance moderate their fortune and prosperity. But if it were so fated, and if now were the time for your good fortune and repose to come to an end, did it have to be by incommoding my king, the very same one by whom you were established? If your house had to fall down in ruins, did it need to fall in its ruin on the hearth of the same man who had embellished it? The thing is so far outside the bounds of reason, so abhorrent to common sense, that it can barely be conceived of by human understanding, and will remain so, incredible to strangers, until the effect, certified and ratified, demonstrates to them that nothing is either holy or sacred to those who have emancipated themselves from God and reason in order to follow their perverse affections.

'If any wrong had been committed by us against your subjects and domains, if any favour had been shown by us to those who wish you ill, if in your affairs we had not come to your aid, if your name and honour had been injured by us; or, to put it more clearly, if the spirit of calumny, endeavouring to lead you into evil, had by false appearances and illusory phantasms put it into your heads that we had done something against you that was not worthy of our former friendship, you ought first to have tried to find out the truth, and then admonished us. And we would have given you all the satisfaction you desired, so you would have had every cause to be content. But (Eternal God!) what are you trying to do? Do you want, like a treacherous tyrant, to go around pillaging and despoiling my master's kingdom in this way? Have you found him to be so cowardly and stupid that he *would* not, or so lacking in soldiers, money, council and military skill that he *could* not, resist your iniquitous assaults?

'Depart hence forthwith, and tomorrow return for good to your own lands, without committing any acts of tumult or violence en route. And pay one thousand gold bezants for the damage you have caused in these lands. One half you will hand over tomorrow, the other half you will pay this coming Ides of May, meanwhile leaving behind as hostages the Dukes of Turnmill, Drooparse and Smallfry, together with the Prince of Scratchem and Viscount Crablouse.

CHAPTER 32
How Grandgousier, to buy peace, had the cakes given back

Whereupon, our friend Gallet fell silent; but the only thing that Picrochole said in reply to all his words was, 'Just come and get 'em! Just come and get 'em! My men have got balls the size of millstones! They'll grind some nice cakes for you!'

So Gallet returned to Grandgousier, whom he found on his knees, head bared, bending over in a little corner of his study, praying God that it be his will to soften Picrochole's anger, and make him see reason again, without having to proceed with forceful means. When he saw his trusty servant had returned, he asked him, 'Friend, ah! my friend, what news have you got for me?'

'The situation is a real mess,' said Gallet. 'The man is out of his mind, and quite godforsaken.'

'I see,' said Grandgousier, 'but tell me, friend, what cause does he claim lay behind his excesses?'

'He didn't tell me of any cause,' said Gallet, 'except that he spoke a few angry words about some cakes. I don't know if there wasn't some insult against his cake-makers.'

'I'm going to find out all about it,' said Grandgousier, 'before I decide what to do.'

So he sent for details of the affair, and found that it was true that a few cakes had been forcibly taken from Picrochole's men, and that Marquet had received a big bang on the noggin. But he learnt that the cakes had all been paid for, and that the aforesaid Marquet had first wounded Forgier by whipping him about his legs. And it seemed to his whole council that he was perfectly justified in defending himself by main force. 'In spite of this,' said Grandgousier, 'since we're only talking about a few cakes, I'll try to content him, since I really don't like the idea of waging war.' So he asked how many cakes they had taken, and when he heard there had been four or five dozen, he ordered them to load up five cartfuls that same night, one of them with cakes made with fine butter, fine egg yolks, fine saffron and fine spices, to be handed over to Marquet; and he would give him as interest 700,003 philips to pay the barbers who had bandaged him, and in addition he gave him the farmstead of La Pomardière as freehold in perpetuity for him and his family. Gallet was chosen to conduct the interview and reach an agreement. On his way there, Gallet stopped by the Willow Grove and ordered that a great supply of bunches of canes and reeds be picked, and had them set around their carts, while each of the carters, and he himself, held one in their hands. By this he wished to demonstrate that they were only after peace, and that they had come to buy it.

When they had reached the gate, they asked to speak to Picrochole on Grandgousier's behalf. Picrochole had no intention of letting them in, nor did he wish to go and speak to them, and he sent a message saying he was busy, but they could say what they wanted to Captain Swashbuckler, who was setting up some cannons on the walls.

And so the good Gallet said to him, 'My Lord, so as to make you drop this quarrel, and remove any pretext for your refusing to return to our former alliance, we are here giving you back the cakes that are the origin of the dispute. Our people took five dozen of them; they paid for them handsomely. We love peace so much that we are giving you five cartloads in return. This one here is for Marquet, who is complaining the most. In addition, so as to satisfy him fully, here are 700,003 philips that I am to hand over; and for any interests he may claim, I am presenting him with the farmstead of La Pomardière in perpetuity for him and his family, freehold. Here is the contract to guarantee the transaction. And for the love of God, let us now live together in peace, and you return merrily home to your own lands, surrendering this place here, where you have absolutely no right to be, as you openly confess. And no hard feelings.'

Swashbuckler related all this to Picrochole, and poisoned his heart more and more, saying, 'Those lubbers have really got the wind up them. By God, Grandgousier is really shitting himself, poor old boozer! He's not made for war, he'd rather drain flagons dry! My opinion is that we grab those cakes and the money, and meanwhile hurry up and fortify this place and see what fortune will bring us. Really! – do they think they're dealing with a complete ninny, if they imagine they can fob you off with a few cakes? I know what's behind it: the kindly treatment and the long familiarity you've shown towards them in the past have bred contempt in them for you. Tender-handed stroke a nettle, And it stings you for your pains; Grasp it like a man of mettle, And it soft as silk remains.'

'Well, well, well!' said Picrochole, 'by St James, that's *just* what they must have been thinking!'

'There's one thing,' said Swashbuckler, 'I'd like to warn you about. We're pretty badly victualled here, and low on supplies of munitions for the belly. If Grandgousier were to lay siege to us, this very minute I'd go and have all my teeth pulled, leaving just three; your soldiers could keep the same number of theirs, too. That would be quite enough teeth for us to eat what provisions we had left.'

'We'll have plenty of grub, and to spare,' said Picrochole. 'Are we here to eat or to do battle?'

'To do battle, of course,' said Swashbuckler. 'But an army marches on its stomach. And where hunger reigns, strength wanes.'

'Stop blathering,' said Picrochole. 'Grab hold of what they've brought.'

So they seized the money and the cakes, and the oxen and the carts, and sent the envoys packing without uttering a single word, merely telling them that they shouldn't come so near again, and they'd tell them why the next day. And so, having accomplished nothing, they returned to Grandgousier and told him all that had happened, adding that there was no hope of persuading them to make peace other than by fierce and open war.

CHAPTER 33

How certain of Picrochole's councillors, by giving him
over-hasty advice, placed him in the utmost danger

When the cakes had been purloined, there appeared before Picrochole the Duke of Smallfry, Count Ruffian and Captain Shitload, who said to him, 'Sire, today we are making you the happiest and most chivalrous prince there has ever been since the death of Alexander of Macedon.'

'Do put your hats on,' said Picrochole.

'Many thanks,' they said. 'Sire, we are merely doing our duty. This is our idea: you will leave here some captain with a small garrison of men to guard the castle, which seems pretty strong to us – both because of its site and because of the ramparts that have been erected in accordance with your plans. You will divide the army into two, as you know only too well how to do. One part will head off and fall upon Grandgousier and his men. He will easily be defeated by them the minute they attack. There, you will pick up heaps of money. The old villain is positively loaded with the stuff. We call him villain because a noble prince never has a penny to his name. To lay up treasure is what villains do. Meanwhile, the other part will head in the direction of Aunis, Saintonge, Angoumois and Gascony, as well as Périgord, Médoc and the Landes. Without encountering any resistance they'll capture towns, châteaux and fortresses. At Bayonne, at Saint-Jean-de-Luz and Fontarabie, you will seize all the ships and, sailing towards Galicia and Portugal, you will pillage all the coastal places until you get to Lisbon, where you will be able to stock up with all the supplies required by a conqueror. By jingo, Spain will surrender – they're nothing but a load of clodhoppers! You'll pass through the Straits of the Sibyl, and there you will erect two columns more magnificent than those of Hercules, in perpetual memory of your name.[131] And this strait will henceforth be known as the Picrocholinian Sea. Once you've crossed the Picrocholinian Sea, hey presto, Barbarossa[132] will surrender, making himself your slave.'

'I,' said Picrochole, 'will show him mercy.'

'Sure you will,' they said, 'so long as he agrees to be baptised. And you will harry the kingdoms of Tunis, Hippo, Algiers, Bona and Cyrene, boldly battling against the whole of Barbary. And going ever further, you will have in your grasp Majorca, Minorca, Sardinia, Corsica and other islands in the Ligurian and Balearic Sea. Skirting the coast on your left, you will hold in thrall the whole of Narbonian Gaul, Provence and the Allobroges, Genoa, Florence, Lucca... and it's goodbye Rome! Poor Mr Pope is already dying with fear.'

'I swear I am *never* going to kiss his slippers,' said Picrochole.

'Once Italy has fallen, lo and behold, Naples, Calabria, Apulia and Sicily will all be sacked, and Malta's in the bag. I'd just like to see those jokers, the knights of Rhodes as they used to be, trying to put up a fight. Then we'd see the colour of their urine.'

'I'd quite like to go to Loretto,' said Picrochole.

'Not now!' they said. 'You can call by on your way back! From there we will take Candia, Cyprus, Rhodes and the Cycladic islands, and fall upon Morea. Gotcha! By St Trinian, may God protect Jerusalem! The Sultan just cannot compete with your power!'

'In that case,' he said, 'I will have Solomon's temple built.'

'Not just yet,' they said. 'Wait a bit. Stop being so hasty in your plans. Do you know what Octavian Augustus used to say? *Festina lente.* First, what you need is to have Asia Minor, Caria, Lycia, Pamphilia, Cilicia, Lydia, Phrygia, Mysia, Bithynia, Carrasia, Satalia, Samagria, Castamena, Luga and Sebasté, right as far as the Euphrates.'

'Will we be able to see Babylon,' asked Picrochole, 'and Mount Sinai?'

'There's no need for that just now,' they said. 'Isn't it enough hassle to have sailed across the Hyrcanian Sea, and galloped across the two Armenias and the three Arabias?'

'Upon my word,' he said, 'we're off our heads! Oh, poor saps that we are!'

'Why?' they said.

'And what exactly are we going to drink in those deserts? Julian Augustus and his whole host died of thirst there, so they say.'[133]

'We have,' they replied, 'ordered all the arrangements to be made. On the Syrian Sea you have 9,014 great ships loaded with the best wines in the world. They've arrived in Jaffa. There, 2,200,000 camels and 1,600 elephants have been assembled – you captured them in a hunt near Sigeilmès, when you entered Libya, and in addition you seized the whole caravan going to Mecca. Didn't they give you all the wine you needed?'

'Well, yes,' he said, 'but we didn't drink it fresh.'

'Ha!' they said, 'not by the virtue of any little fish! – a valiant knight, a conqueror, a claimant and aspirant to the empire of the whole world can't always have an easy life. God be praised that you have reached – you and your troops – the River Tigris, safe and sound.'

'But,' said he, 'what's the part of our army that defeated that boozy old villain Grandgousier been getting up to in the meantime?'

'They're not being lazy,' they said, 'we'll be meeting up with them soon. They've captured Brittany for you, and Normandy, Flanders, Hainaut, Brabant, Artois, Holland and Zeeland; they've crossed the Rhine over the stomachs of the Swiss and the Lansquenets, and a detachment of them has overrun Luxembourg, Lorraine, Champagne and Savoy as far as Lyons, where they found your garrisons returning from their naval conquests in the Mediterranean Sea. And they re-assembled in Bohemia, after sacking Swabia, Württemberg, Bavaria, Austria, Moravia and Styria. Then they fell fiercely together on Lübeck, Norway, the Kingdom of Sweden, Dacia, Goetaland, Greenland and the Easterlings[134], right up to the Glacial Sea. After this, they conquered the Orkneys, and subjugated Scotland, England and Ireland. From there, they sailed across the Sandy Sea, and crossed the Sarmatians, from where they conquered and imposed their rule on Prussia, Poland, Lithuania, Russia, Wallachia, Transylvania and Hungary, Bulgaria, Turkey, and they've reached Constantinople.'

'Let's catch up with them,' said Picrochole, 'as quick as we can – I want to be Emperor of Trebizond too! Won't we just slaughter all those Turkish and Mohammadist dogs?'

'And what the devil will we do then?' they asked. 'Anyway, you will give their lands and property to those who have served you honourably.'

'Reason wills it!' he said. 'It's only fair. I give you Carmania, Syria and the whole of Palestine.'

'Ah!' they said, 'Sire, that's so kind of you! Thanks very much! May God grant you a long and prosperous life!'

There was with them an old gentleman who had experienced many dangers, a real old warhorse called Echephron[135]. Hearing these words, he said, 'I'm very much afraid this enterprise may turn out like the farcical story of the milk jug, which a shoemaker dreamt was going to make him rich; then, when the jug got broken, he didn't have anything to eat for dinner.[136] What is the aim of all these fine conquests? What will be the end of so many labours and travels?'

'Well,' said Picrochole, 'it will be nice when we get back home and can relax.'

To which Echephron replied, 'And what if by chance you *didn't* get back home? The journey is a long and perilous one. Wouldn't it be better for us to relax right now, without having to run all those risks?'

'Oh!' said Ruffian, 'by God, what a dozy dreamer we have here! Let's all go and huddle by the fireside; and there we can spend our lives with our ladies, passing the time stringing pearls or spinning like Sardanapalus![137] He who risks nothing has neither horse nor mule, as Solomon says.'

'He who risks too much,' replied Echephron, 'loses both horse and mule, as Marcon retorts.'[138]

'Shut up!' said Picrochole. 'Let's go further. All I fear is those devilish legions of Grandgousier's. While we are in Mesopotamia, if they fell upon our rear, what could we do?'

'There's an easy solution,' said Shitload, 'a nice little commission you will issue to the Muscovites will bring into your camp, in a flash, 450,000 crack troops. Oh! If only you'll make me your lieutenant, I'd kill a comb for a haberdasher. I bite, I charge, I strike, I catch, I kill!'

'Up and away!' said Picrochole. 'Make haste! And he who loves me, let him follow me!'

CHAPTER 34

How Gargantua left the city of Paris to come to the aid of his country;
and how Gymnast met the enemy

At this very same time, Gargantua, who had left Paris the moment he had read his father's letter, riding on his great mare, had already passed the Nun's Bridge – he, Ponocrates, Gymnast and Eudemon, who had taken post horses to follow him. The rest of his retinue came along at a slower pace, a day at a time, bringing all his books and philosophical instruments.

When he had arrived at Parillé, he was alerted by the farmer of Gouguet as to how Picrochole had fortified himself in La Roche Clermaud, and had sent Captain Tripet, with a great army, to attack the Wood of Vède, and Vagaudry, and that they had been hunting down every last chicken all the way to the winepress at Billard, and it was a strange and difficult thing to believe how great were the ravages they were inflicting on the whole region. The farmer's account was so vivid that it frightened Gargantua, and he didn't really know what to say or do. But Ponocrates advised him that they should make their way to the Lord of La Vauguyon, who had always been their friend and confederate, and he would be able to give them a more accurate picture of the whole situation. This they did straight away, and found that he was quite prepared to come to their aid. And it was his opinion that he should send one of his men to reconnoitre the area and find out what state the enemy were in, so as to proceed with all due caution, depending on how things turned out at this present moment. Gymnast offered to go himself, but it was decided that it would be better for him to take along someone who knew what route to follow and how to avoid wrong turnings, and who was acquainted with all the local rivers.

So off they set, he and Sprightly, the Squire of Vauguyon, and they fearlessly spied out the lie of the land on every side. Meanwhile, Gargantua stopped to rest and have a bite to eat with his men, and gave his mare a peck of oats – seventy-four hogsheads and three bushels' worth.

Gymnast and his companion rode along until they met the enemy, scattered around in disorder, pillaging and robbing everything they could. And while Gymnast was still in the distance, they spotted him, and came running up to him in a great unruly crowd, ready to rob him.

Then he shouted to them, 'Gentlemen, I'm a poor devil, I beg you show me mercy! I've still got a crown or so left on me. Let's all have a drink, it's *aurum potabile*[139]; and this horse here can be sold to pay for my welcome. After that, you can retain my services. I'll happily join you – there was never a man better at catching, larding, roasting and preparing, not to mention (by God!) dismembering and guzzling a chicken than yours truly, in person! And for my *proficiat*, I drink to all my good friends.'

Whereupon he uncovered his canteen and, without dipping his nose in it, drank quite politely. The rascals watched him, opening their mouths a foot wide, their tongues hanging out like greyhounds waiting for their turn to drink. But Tripet, their captain, came running up just then to see what all the fuss was about. Then Gymnast offered him his bottle, saying, 'Here you are, captain, don't hold back, have a nice drink! I've tried it. It's wine from La Faye Monjau.'

'What's this?' said Tripet. 'Is this oaf here taking the piss out of us? Who d'you think you are?'

'I'm just a poor devil,' said Gymnast.

'Ha!' said Tripet, 'since you're just a poor devil, you've got every reason to pass on your way, for any poor devil can pass wherever he wants without paying tolls or duties. But it's not usual for poor devils to be so well mounted. And so, Mr Devil, come down so that I can have your old carthorse; and if he doesn't carry me properly, *you* can carry me instead, Master Devil! I'm really happy for a devil like you to give me a lift!'

CHAPTER 35
How Gymnast nimbly killed Captain Tripet,
and some of Picrochole's other soldiers

On hearing these words, some of them started to feel alarmed, and made the sign of the cross with every hand available, thinking he must be a devil in disguise. And one of them, Old John by name, Captain of the

Rural Militia, pulled out his breviary from his codpiece, and cried in a pretty loud voice, '*Hagios ho theos*,[140] if you come from God, then speak! If you come from the other one, then go away!' And he didn't go away, which several in the gang noted, whereupon they left the company – while Gymnast observed and reflected on all these proceedings.

Therefore, he pretended to be climbing down off his horse, and when he was hanging on the side where you climb up, he nimbly performed the stirrup trick, with his short sword at his side, and having swung himself underneath his horse, threw himself up into the air and stood with both feet on the saddle, his backside turned towards the horse's head. Then he said, 'Arse and elbow have changed places!' Then, in the position he was in, he leapt up on one foot, did a left turn, and successfully came back to his original position without varying a hand's breadth from it. At which Tripet exclaimed, 'Ha! That's not a move I'm going to make right now. I have plenty of reasons not to.'

'Shit,' said Gymnast, 'I got it wrong. I'm going to undo that leap.'

Then, using great strength and agility, he performed the same leap as before, only this time to the right. Then, he placed the thumb of his right hand on the pommel of his saddle and lifted up his whole body, supporting his whole body on the muscles and sinews of the said thumb; and in this position he turned round three times. On the fourth time, twisting his whole body backwards without touching anything, he sat bolt upright between his horse's two ears, holding his whole body in the air on the thumb of his left hand; and in this position he performed the 'windmill', then, striking the palm of his right hand on the middle of the saddle, he gave himself enough momentum to sit on the crupper, as ladies do. Then, with perfect ease he passed his right leg over the saddle, and got himself ready to ride along, on the crupper. 'But,' he said, 'it would be better for me to sit between the saddle-bows.' And so, propping himself up with the thumbs of both hands on the crupper in front of him, he did a somersault, arse over tip, and found himself between the saddle-bows in perfect posture, then with another somersault lifted his whole body into the air, and in this way held himself with his feet together between the saddle-bows, and there did over a hundred turns, his arms held out crossways, and as he did so he bellowed out, 'I'm mad with anger, devils! Mad, quite mad! Catch me if you can, devils! Catch me! Catch!'

While he was performing these tricks on horseback, the rascals were all standing there in amazement, saying to each other, 'By Our Lady of Muck! He's a goblin, or a devil in disguise! *Ab hoste maligno, libera nos, domine*.'[141] And they fled down the road, looking behind them, like a dog carrying off a chicken wing from the kitchen.

Then Gymnast, seeing his advantage, got off his horse and unsheathed his sword, and swiping out left and right he charged at the ones that seemed the most dangerous, and knocked them down in great heaps of wounded, injured and bruised, without any of them putting up any resistance, as they thought he must be a famished devil, both because of the wonderful horseback tricks he had performed and because of the things Tripet had said to him, calling him 'poor devil'. The exception was Tripet himself, who treacherously tried to split his skull with his lansquenet's sword. But Gymnast was well armoured, and all he felt of this blow was the bare impetus of it; and immediately turning round, he feinted at the said Tripet, and while the latter was protecting his upper body, with one blow slashed through his stomach, his colon and half his liver. Whereupon he fell to the ground, and as he fell he threw up more than four potfuls of soup, and his soul came out mingled with the soup.

After this, Gymnast retired from the fray, considering that one should never pursue chance advantages to their limit, and that it is proper for all knights to treat their good fortune with reverence, not straining it or forcing it too violently. And, climbing onto his horse, he dug his spurs in and headed straight off to La Vauguyon, with Sprightly at his side.

CHAPTER 36
How Gargantua demolished the château at the Ford of Vède; and how they crossed the ford

As soon as he was back, he described the state in which he had found the enemy, and the stratagem he had used – he alone against all their troop – saying that they were nothing but rogues, pillagers and brigands, ignorant of all military discipline; Gargantua and his men should set out boldly, as it would be extremely easy to slaughter the enemy like cattle.

So Gargantua climbed onto his great mare, accompanied by his retinue as we said earlier. And finding in his path a huge tall tree (which was generally called St Martin's tree, because a pilgrim's staff had grown there that St Martin had once planted), he said, 'This is just what I needed. This tree will serve me as both pilgrim's staff and lance.' And he easily wrenched it out of the ground and stripped it of its branches, and trimmed it in the way that best pleased him. Meanwhile, his mare had pissed to take the weight off her belly, but the flow was so abundant that she caused a flood for seven leagues around; and the stream of piss flowed down into the Ford of Vède, and, going against the current, made it swell so much that the whole band of enemies were drowned, dying most horribly, apart from a few who had taken the road towards the hill slopes on the left.

Gargantua, on reaching the Wood of Vède, was alerted by Eudemon to the fact that inside the château there were still a few enemy soldiers. To find out the exact situation, Gargantua shouted at the top of his voice, 'Are you there or aren't you? If you *are* there, don't stay there; if you *aren't* there, I've nothing more to say.' But a cheeky cannoneer standing at the machicolations let off a cannon shot at him, which struck him a furious blow on the right temple. All the same, it didn't hurt him any more than if the man had thrown a plum at him.

'What's this?' said Gargantua. 'Are you starting to throw grape pips at us? The harvest is going to cost you dear' (he thought that the cannonball actually *was* a grape pip). Those who were in the château intent on pillage heard the noise and ran out onto the towers and fortresses, and fired more than 9,025 falcons and harquebuses, all aimed directly at his head; and they fired so thick and fast at him, that he exclaimed, 'Ponocrates, my friend, all these flies are blinding me! Give me one of the branches from those willows, so I can shoo them away' (he thought that the lead cannonballs and artillery stones were gadflies). Ponocrates advised him that the only flies around were the artillery shots being fired from the château. Then he battered the château with his great tree, and with mighty blows knocked down

93

the towers and the fortresses, and razed the building to the ground in its entirety. In this way all those who were inside were crushed and smashed to pieces.

From there they moved on to the mill bridge, and found the entire ford strewn with dead bodies, such a crowd of them that they had choked up the millstream; and these were the men who had perished in the flood of urine from the mare. This made them halt and reflect on how they could get across, in view of the fact that these corpses were blocking the way. But Gymnast said, 'If the devils have got across, then I'll easily do so.'

'The devils,' said Eudemon, 'have got across so as to carry away the damned souls.'

'By St Trinian!' said Ponocrates, 'then it's a logical consequence that *he'll* necessarily be able to get across.'

'Yes, indeed,' said Gymnast, 'or else I'll get stuck halfway across.' And sticking his spurs into his horse, he easily passed over, without his horse being in the slightest alarmed by the dead bodies, since he had trained him (following the teaching of Aelian[142]) not to fear souls, nor dead bodies. He'd done this not by killing lots of people, in the way Diomedes killed the Thracians, or the way Ulysses placed the bodies of his enemies in front of the feet of his horses, as Homer relates, but by putting a scarecrow in his hay, and making the horse get used to trampling over it when he gave him his oats. The three others followed him unflinchingly, except for Eudemon, whose horse sank its right foot down right up to the knee in the belly of a big fat rogue who was lying there on his back, drowned; and the horse couldn't get its leg out, but remained stuck there, until Gargantua used the end of his stick to push the rest of the rogue's tripes away into the water, while the horse tugged its foot out. And (something quite wonderful in the annals of hippiatry[143]), the said horse was cured of a ringbone it had on the very same foot, thanks to the touch of that great oaf's bowels.

CHAPTER 37
How Gargantua, combing his hair, caused artillery shells to come tumbling out of it

They left the bank of the Vède and shortly thereafter reached Grand-gousier's château, where everyone was waiting for them in a state of eager anticipation. On Gargantua's arrival, they threw a huge banquet to celebrate: never did you see people more joyous. Indeed, the *Supplementum supplementi chronicorum*[144] says that Gargamelle died of joy during it. For my part, I haven't the slightest idea, and I couldn't care less either about her or about anybody else.

The truth of the matter was that Gargantua, while putting on clean clothes and giving his hair a lick with his comb (which was a hundred canes long, and set with enormous unbroken elephants' teeth), at each stroke caused more than seven artillery shells that had got caught in his hair during the demolition of the Wood of Vède to come tumbling out. On seeing this, his father, Grandgousier, thought they must be lice and said to him, 'Good Lord, my son, have you brought us back some sparrowhawks all the way from Montaigu?[145] I didn't think you'd taken up residence there.'

Then Ponocrates replied, 'My Lord, don't think for a minute that I placed him in that lousy college they call Montaigu. I'd much rather have sent him to school with the beggars of Saint-Innocent[146], given the horrific cruelty and sordidness that I encountered there. You can bet that galley slaves are far better treated among the Moors and Tartars, murderers in the criminals' gaol, or even, to be sure, dogs in your house, than are those poor bumpkins in the aforesaid college. And if I were king of Paris, devil take me but I'd set fire to the place and burn up the principal and the lecturers who are prepared to put up with this inhumanity being committed right in front of their very own eyes.'

Then, lifting one of the shells, he said, 'They're cannonballs that were fired at your son, Gargantua, just now, when he was making his way past the Wood of Vède – a treacherous attack by your enemies. But they got their just deserts: they all perished in the ruin of the château, like the Philistines by the cunning of Samson, and those who were crushed by the Tower of Siloam, of whom it is written in Luke XIII. In my opinion, we should pursue those men while we have luck on our side. Opportunity has all its hair in front, and once it has passed you by, you'll never have another chance to lay hold of it; it's bald at the back of its head, and never turns round for you.'

'True,' said Grandgousier, 'but not right now – I want to give you a splendid banquet this evening. I wish you all most welcome!'

On these words, supper was prepared, and in addition there were roasted sixteen oxen, three heifers, thirty-two calves, sixty-three suckling kids, ninety-five sheep, three hundred suckling pigs with a nice sour wine sauce, eleven score partridges, seven hundred woodcocks, four hundred capons from Loudun and Cornouaille, six thousand chickens and the same number of pigeons, six hundred guinea hens, fourteen hundred leverets, three hundred and three bustards, and one thousand seven hundred young capons. When it came to venison, in such a short time they were unable to rustle up quite so much – just eleven boars, sent by the Abbot of Turpenay, and eighteen fallow deer given by the Lord of Grandmont, together with seven score pheasants sent by the Lord des Essars, and several dozen turtle doves, river birds, teal, bitterns, curlews, plovers, grouse, young lapwings, sheldrakes, black and white waterfowl, spoonbills, herons, young coots and grown coots, egrets, storks, land fowl, orange flamingos (phenicopters[147], in other words), corncrakes, turkeys, loads of couscous and plenty of broth. Make no mistake – there were victuals in abundance, and they were very nicely prepared by Licksauce, Hotpot and Pestlevinegar, Grandgousier's cooks. Johnny, Mike and Drainyourglass laid on an excellent supply of drinks.

CHAPTER 38
How Gargantua ate six pilgrims in a salad

The story requires that we now relate what happened to six pilgrims who came from Saint-Sébastien near Nantes, and in order to find shelter that night had hunkered down, for fear of the enemy, in the garden, on the pea stalks between the cabbages and the lettuces.

Gargantua was feeling a bit thirsty and asked if they could fetch some lettuces to make him a salad. And on hearing that there were some of the biggest and most splendid in the country, as big as plum trees or walnut trees, he decided to go himself and brought back in his hand as many as he wanted. And with them he also picked up the six pilgrims, who were so afraid that they didn't dare either speak or cough. So, as he was first washing them in the fountain, the pilgrims were muttering in low voices to one another, 'Whatever are we going to do? We're drowning here, among these lettuces – shall we say something? But if we do, he'll kill us as spies.'

And as they were deliberating in this way, Gargantua put them with his lettuces into one of the dishes in his house, as big as the cask of Cîteaux, and having added oil, vinegar and salt, he ate them to refresh himself before his supper, and in no time he'd already swallowed five of the pilgrims.

The sixth was inside the dish, hidden under a lettuce – apart from his pilgrim's staff, which poked out from underneath. When Grandgousier saw this, he said to Gargantua, 'I think that's a snail's horn, don't eat it.'

'Why not?' said Gargantua. 'They're good all this month.'

And pulling out the staff, he lifted up the pilgrim at the same time and heartily devoured him. Then he drank a horrific great draught of Pinot wine, and waited for his supper to be prepared.

The pilgrims who had been devoured in this way did their best to escape from his great grinding teeth, and thought that someone must have put them into some deep dark dungeon. And when Gargantua drank his great draught, they thought they were going to drown in his mouth, and the torrent of wine almost swept them away down into the chasm of his stomach. However, by jumping up with the help of their staffs in the way pilgrims to Mont-Saint-Michel do, they managed to find shelter on the outskirts of his teeth.

But unfortunately, one of them, tapping all around with his staff to find if they were safe, prodded it roughly into the cavity of a hollow tooth and struck the nerve in the jawbone. This gave Gargantua a very sharp pain and he started to bellow with the agony he was thus forced to endure. And in order to relieve the pain, he had his toothpick

97

brought and, going outside to where the walnut tree stood, the one with such hard nuts that only crows can break them open, he managed to extract my lords the pilgrims. He caught one by the legs, another by the shoulders, the other by the knapsack, the other by the wallet, the other by the scarf; and the poor wretch who'd hit him with his staff he caught up by his codpiece. However, this was a piece of great good fortune for him, as he pierced a nasty sore that had been tormenting him ever since the time they had passed Ancenis. In this way, the pilgrims who had been extracted fled across the newly planted vines as fast as their legs could carry them, and the pain subsided.

At that moment, Eudemon called him in to supper, as everything was ready. 'I'm just off,' he said, 'to piss away my misfortune.' And he pissed in such torrents that the urine cut off the pilgrims' path, and they were forced to wade through the great stream as through a canal. From there they passed along the edge of La Touche Wood, where all of them, apart from Fournillier, fell into a great trap in the middle of the road, set there to catch wolves in its net. But they escaped thanks to the ingenuity of the said Fournillier, who managed to break all the ropes and snares.

Having struggled out, for the rest of that night they slept in a hut near Le Coudray. And there they were given solace for their misfortune by the fine words of one of their company, a man called Slowcoach, who pointed out to them that this adventure had been predicted by David, Ps. *Cum exurgerent homines in nos, forte vivos deglutissent nos,*[148] when we were eaten in a salad with a pinch of salt. *Cum irasceretur furor eorum in nos, forsitan aqua absorbuisset nos,*[149] when he drank the great draught. *Torrentem pertransivit anima nostra,* when we passed through the great stream, *forsitan pertransisset anima nostra, aquam intolerabilem,*[150] of his urine, with which he cut off our path. *Benedictus dominus qui non dedit nos in captionem dentibus eorum. Anima nostra sicut passer erepta est de laqueo vanentium,*[151] when we fell into the trap. *Laqueus contritus est,* by Fournillier, *et nos liberati sumus. Adjutorium nostrum, etc.*'[152]

CHAPTER 39
How the Monk was feasted by Gargantua;
and the lively remarks he made at supper

When Gargantua was at table and the first course of hors d'oeuvres had been wolfed down, Grandgousier started to recount the origin and cause of the war being waged between himself and Picrochole; when he reached the point where he had to tell of how Brother John of the Mincemeat had triumphed in his defence of the abbey close, he praised his deed above all the feats of arms of Camillus, Scipio, Pompey, Caesar and Themistocles. Then Gargantua requested them to go and fetch him straight away, so that they could consult with him on what to do. At their bidding, the maître d' went to find him and brought him merrily back, with his staff and cross, on Grandgousier's mule.

Once he had arrived, they hugged and embraced and said hello to each other thousands of times. 'Hey, Brother John, old pal! Brother John, my great cousin! Brother John, devil take it, come and give me a big hug! Come on, throw your arms round me! Come on, you old bollocky fellow, let me squeeze you flat with my embraces!' And Brother John laughed his head off. Never was a man more courteous or more gracious.

'Come on, then!' said Gargantua. 'Draw up a stool here, right next to me, at this end of the table.'

'That's fine by me,' said the Monk, 'if that's the way you want it. Pageboy, a little water. Pour it out, lad, pour it out! It'll refresh my liver. Come on, more, enough for me to wash my mouth out!'

'*Deposita cappa*,' said Gargantua, 'let's take this gown off.'

'Hey, by God!' said the Monk. 'My dear fellow, there's a chapter *in statutis ordinis*[153] that wouldn't be very happy with that.'

'Shit!' said Gymnast. 'Shit on your chapter! This gown is weighing down both your shoulders. Take it off.'

'My friend,' said the Monk, 'let me keep it on. After all, by God, it helps me drink all the more. It makes my body all frisky. If I leave it off, my lords, the pageboys will turn it into garters, as once happened to me at Coulaines. What's more, I'll lose my appetite. But if I sit down to table while wearing this habit, I'll drink, by God, both to you and to your horse! And with all my heart!

'God protect the company from evil! I'd already had supper, but that won't stop me eating any the less. You see, I have a stomach that's well paved, as hollow as St Benedict's great barrel, always open like a lawyer's game bag. From every fish except the tench, take the partridge's wing or a nun's thigh. Isn't dying droll when you die with a stiff prick? Our prior is very fond of white capon meat.'

'In that respect,' said Gymnast, 'he's quite different from foxes – when they catch capons, hens and chickens, they never eat the white.'

'Why?' said the Monk.

'Because,' replied Gymnast, 'they don't have a cook to cook them. And if they're not completely cooked, they stay red, not white. The redness of meats is the sign that they aren't cooked enough. The exception is lobsters and crayfish, which are cardinalised by cooking.'

'Corpus Christi! – as Bayard used to say,'[154] remarked the Monk, 'the hospitaller of our abbey can't have a head that's well cooked, since his eyes are as red as a bowl of alderwood. This thigh of leveret is good for gout sufferers. Changing the subject, why is it that the thighs of a lady are always cool?'

'That problem,' said Gargantua, 'is neither in Aristotle, nor in Alex. Aphrodisias, nor in Plutarch.'

'It's for three reasons,' said the Monk, 'that a place is naturally kept cool. Firstly, because water trickles along it. Secondly, because it's a shady, dim, dark place into which the sun never shines. And thirdly, because it is continually ventilated by a breeze from the North Hole, as well as from the flapping of shirts and, in addition, the wagging of codpieces. Ah, how lovely! Pageboy, another drink! Clink, clink, clink! How gracious is God, who gives us this fine wine! I swear to God, if I'd been around at the time of Jesus Christ, I'd have made sure the Jews didn't catch him in the Garden of Olivet! What's more, devil take me but I'd have made sure I hamstrung my lords the Apostles, who fled in such a cowardly way after they'd enjoyed such a nice supper, and left their good master in the lurch. I hate more than poison any man who flees when it's time for some knife play. Ha! If only I were king of France for eighty or a hundred years! By God, I'd cut off the ears and tails of those dogs who fled at Pavia![155] May they be stricken with ague! Why couldn't they die there rather than leaving their prince in such a plight?

Isn't it better and more honourable to die valiantly fighting, than to live by running away like a despicable wretch? We won't be eating many goslings this year. Ah, my friend, hand over a slice of that pork! Damn it, there's no more must![156] Needs must when the devil rides. *Germinavit radix Jesse.*[157] Just look – no wine! I don't want to sound whiny but… I thirst. I'm dying of it! This wine isn't bad. What wine did you drink in Paris? Devil take me if I didn't keep a house there, open to all and sundry, for more than six months. Did you happen to know Brother Claude des Hauts Barrois? Oh, he's a great pal to have! But what exactly has got into him? He's done nothing but study ever since I dunno when! I don't study, personally speaking. In our abbey we never study, in case we catch the mumps. Our late abbot used to say that a learned monk is a monstrous sight. By God, my esteemed friend, *magis magnos clericos non sunt magis magnos sapientes.*[158] You never saw so many hares as there've been this year. I haven't been able to get a goshawk or a tassel, though I've looked everywhere. Monsieur de la Bellonnière had promised me a lanner, but he wrote to me a while ago to tell me it had fallen ill. The partridges will eat our ears off this year, yeah! I don't much enjoy fowling with a tunnel net – I always get cold. Unless I'm running and kicking up a shindy, I'm not at my ease. It's true that, jumping over hedgerows and bushes as I do, my gown leaves hairs behind. I caught a really nice hare. Devil take me if a single hare escapes. A lackey was taking him round to Monsieur de Maulevrier: I stole it off him. Hare today, gone tomorrow. Was I wrong to do so?'

'Not at all!' said Gymnast. 'No, Brother John, no, by all the devils, no!'

'Well then,' said the Monk, 'here's to all those devils, for as long as they last! God Almighty, what would old hopalong have done with it? Jeepers, he's happier when someone gives him a nice pair of oxen.'

'What's this?' said Ponocrates. 'Are you swearing, Brother John?'

'It's just to titivate my language a bit,' said the Monk. 'These are the colours of Ciceronian rhetoric.'

CHAPTER 40
Why monks are shunned by everyone;
and why some people have bigger noses than others

'Upon my word as a Christian,' said Eudemon, 'I'm really starting to be quite amazed at what a thoroughly decent chap this monk here is. He's giving us all such a laugh. So how come monks are always thrown out of all good company, and called spoilsports, in the same way that bees chase drones from around their hives? *Ignavum fucos pecus*, as Virgil says, *a presepibus arcent.*'[159]

Gargantua replied, 'It's perfectly true that a monk's robe and cowl draw on their wearer the opprobrium, insults and curses of the whole world, just as the wind called Caecias attracts clouds. The most compelling reason is that they eat the world's shit, i.e. its sins, and since they are shit-eaters, they are forced back into their privies, in other words their monasteries and abbeys, kept away from polite conversation just as the privies in a house are kept apart from the rest. But if you can understand why a monkey in a family is always mocked and made fun of, you can understand why monks are shunned by everyone young and old. The monkey doesn't guard the house, like a dog; it doesn't draw the plough, like an ox; it doesn't produce milk, or wool, like a ewe; it doesn't bear burdens, like a horse. What the monkey does is to make a shitty mess everywhere and spoil everything, and this is the reason why he is the butt of everyone's mockery and is always getting beaten by them. Likewise, a monk (one of those idle monks, I mean) doesn't toil in the fields, like a peasant; doesn't guard his country, like a man of war; doesn't heal the sick, like a doctor; doesn't preach or instruct the world in doctrine, like a good evangelical preacher and teacher; doesn't carry the commodities and things necessary to the commonwealth, like a merchant. That's the reason why monks are hooted at and hated by everyone.'

'Yes, but,' said Grandgousier, 'they do pray to God for us.'

'They do no such thing,' said Gargantua. 'It's true that they disturb their whole neighbourhood by dingdonging their bells.'

('Yes, but,' said the Monk, 'mass and matins and vespers, when well rung, are already half sung.')

'They mutter,' continued Gargantua, 'a great load of legends and psalms that they don't understand the least little bit. They recite plenty of paternosters, interlarded with long Ave Marias, without concentrating on what they're saying or understanding any of it. And this I call God-mockery, not prayer. But may God help them if they really do pray for us, and not just for fear of losing their loaves and rich soups. All true Christians, of every condition, in every place, at every time, pray to God, and the spirit prays and makes intercession for them, and God takes them into his mercy.

'Now then, our friend Brother John isn't like those other monks at all. That's why everyone wants his company. He's not bigoted, he doesn't dress like an old tramp; he's a decent chap, cheerful, resolute, a real good friend. He works, he labours, he defends the oppressed, he comforts the afflicted, he comes to the aid of the suffering, he guards the abbey close.'

'I do a lot more than that!' said the Monk. 'While dispatching our matins and anniversaries in the choir, I also make crossbow strings, I polish the great bolts and quarrels for them, I make nets and pouches to catch rabbits. I'm never lazy. But anyway, what about another drink, hey? Over here! Bring the fruit! Chestnuts from the Estrocs Wood. With some nice new wine, you'll soon be a fine composer of farts! Aren't you lot in here tiddly yet? By God, I drink at every ford, like a proctor's horse!'

Gymnast said to him, 'Brother John, there's a big bogey hanging on your nose, wipe it away!'

'Ha!' said the Monk, 'could I be in danger of drowning, seeing that I'm in water up to my nose? No way. *Quare? Quia*[160] water comes out of me all right, but none of it goes in. You see, it's well antidoted with vine leaves. Oh, my friend, anyone with winter boots made of leather like this would be able to venture out oyster-fishing. His boots would never let the water in.'

'Why is it,' asked Gargantua, 'that Brother John has such a fine nose?'

'Because,' replied Grandgousier, 'God so willed it, God who fashions us in the shape and with the purpose that his divine judgement has ordained, just as a potter shapes his vessels.'

'Because,' said Ponocrates, 'he was one of the first to get to the nose market. He chose the finest and biggest of them.'

'Come off it!' said the Monk. 'According to authentic monastic philosophy, it's because my nurse had soft tits. As I suckled her, my nose sank right in, as if into butter, and there it rose and swelled like dough in the kneading trough. When nurses have hard titties, they make children snub-nosed. But cheers anyway! *ad formam nasi cognoscitur ad te levavi.*[161] I never eat sweets. Page, keep an eye on our glasses! And ditto the toasted snacks!'

CHAPTER 41
How the Monk sent Gargantua to sleep; and details of his breviary hours

When supper was over, they consulted on the situation facing them, and it was decided that around midnight they would go out reconnoitring to discover what watch and guard their enemy was keeping. In the meantime, they would rest a while, so as to be fresher.

But Gargantua couldn't sleep, no matter how hard he tried. So the Monk said to him, 'I never sleep properly except when I'm listening to a sermon or praying to God. I beg you, let's you and me together begin the Seven Psalms, to see if you soon won't be fast asleep.' Gargantua was highly pleased with this novel idea. And, starting the first psalm, as soon as they reached the *Beati quorum*,[162] they both dropped off to sleep.

But the Monk never failed to wake before midnight, so used was he to the time matins was sung in the cloister. Once he was awake, he woke all the others, bellowing at the top of his voice the song, 'Ho, Regnault, it's wakey-wakey time! Oh, Regnault, it's time to wake up!' When they were all awake, he said, 'Gentlemen, they say that matins begins with coughing, and supper with drinking. Let's do it the other way round: let's start matins now with a drink, and this evening, when supper is brought in, we'll all see who can cough the most.'

Gargantua replied, 'Drinking so soon after sleep? This isn't what the doctor ordered. First you have to scour your stomach clean of its superfluities and excrements.'

'Fine medical advice that is!' said the Monk. 'A hundred devils jump on my body if there aren't more old drunkards than old doctors! I've come to an agreement with my appetite. We've made a pact – it always goes to bed with me, and I make all the necessary arrangements for it during the day, and so it gets up with me too. *You* can look after your castings if that's what you want – I'm going after my tiring.'[163]

'What tiring do you mean?' said Gargantua.

'My breviary,' said the Monk. 'Just as falconers, before feeding their birds, make them tire on some hen's foot to purge their brains of phlegm and give them an appetite, in the same way I take this merry little breviary in my hand, and with it I scour out my lungs, and lo and behold, I'm ready to drink.'

'Which version of these fine breviary hours do you use?' asked Gargantua.

'The Fécamp version,'[164] said the Monk, 'the one with three psalms and three lessons, or nothing at all, if that's what people want. I never observe the hours submissively. Hours are made for man, and not man for hours. And so I recite my hours stirrup-style: I shorten them or lengthen them as I see fit. *Brevis oratio penetrat celos, longa potatio evacuat scyphos.*[165] Where's that written?'

'I swear I don't know,' said Ponocrates, 'I don't know, you old bollocks, but you really are priceless!'

'Then I'm like you,' said the Monk. 'But *Venite apotemus.*'[166]

They prepared carbonadoes aplenty and some nice soup for primes, and the Monk drank to his heart's content. Some kept him company, while others declined. Afterwards, each of them began to arm and accoutre themselves. And they armed the Monk against his will, as the only weapons he really wanted were his habit in front of his stomach and his staff and cross in his fist. Still, to please them he was armed cap-à-pie, and mounted on a fine steed of the realm, with a great brackmard at his side, together with Gargantua, Ponocrates, Gymnast, Eudemon and twenty-five of the boldest fellows in Grandgousier's household, all well armed, lance in hand, mounted like St George, each of them with a harquebus on the crupper of his horse.

CHAPTER 42

How the Monk gave fresh heart to his companions;
and how he was left hanging from a tree

And so off they head, those noble champions in quest of adventure, fully resolved to discover what encounter they must seek, and what they will need to guard against when comes the day of the great and terrible battle. And the Monk gives them fresh heart, saying, 'Have no fear or hesitation, lads! I'll lead you safely. May God and St Benedict be with us! If I had as much strength as I have courage, by Jiminy, I'd pluck them for you like a duck! I fear nothing, apart from the artillery. Still, there's a prayer I know that was told me by the under-sacristan of our abbey, which guarantees one against all firearms. But it won't be of any use to me, as I don't have the slightest faith in it. Still, my staff and cross will do devilish good work. By God, if any of you lot should duck, devil take me if I don't make him into a monk instead of me, and wrap him in my habit! It's good medicine for people suffering from cowardice. Haven't you heard of the greyhound of Monsieur de Meurles, who was no use at all in the open fields? He put a monk's habit round his neck; by Jeepers, not a hare or a fox could get away from him, and, what's more, he mounted all the bitches in the area, despite having been impotent, and *de frigidis et maleficiatis*.'[167]

As the Monk was speaking these words in anger, he passed under a walnut tree, as he was heading in the direction of the Willow Grove, and caught the visor of his helm on the sharp end of a great broken branch of the tree. In spite of this, he fiercely dug his spurs into his horse, who was sensitive to pricks, so that the horse leapt forward, and the Monk, trying to extricate his visor from the hook of the branch, dropped the bridle and hung by his hand from the branches, while the horse galloped away from under him.

In this way, the Monk remained hanging from the walnut tree, shouting out 'Help!' and 'Murder!' and protesting something about 'treachery!' too. Eudemon was the first to notice him. And calling Gargantua, he said, 'Sire, come over here, and see Absalom hanged!'[168] Gargantua came up, took a long look at the Monk's face and the way he was hanging, and said to Eudemon, 'You've not got it right, comparing him to Absalom. Absalom was hanged by the hair, but the Monk, who has a shaven pate, has hanged himself by the ears.'

'Help me,' said the Monk, 'for the devil's sake! Do you really think this is the time to stand round nattering? You remind me of Decretalist preachers, who say that anyone who sees his neighbour in danger of death must on pain of triple excommunication urge him to confess his sins and put himself in a state of grace, rather than help him.[169] So if one day I see those preachers have fallen into the river and are on the point of drowning, instead of going to help them and giving them a hand, I'll deliver a nice long sermon *de contemptu mundi et fuga seculi*;[170] and when they're stone dead, *then* I'll fish them out!'

'Don't move, sweety!' said Gymnast, 'I'm coming for you – you're such a nice little *monachus*:

> '*Monachus in claustro*
> *Non valet ova duo;*
> *Sed quando est extra,*
> *Bene valet triginta.*[171]

'I've seen hanged men, more than five hundred of them,' he continued, 'but I've never seen anyone who dangled there more gracefully; and if I could dangle as well as that, I'd spend my whole life hanging there.'

'Haven't you preached enough by now?' said the Monk. 'Help me, for God's sake, since you won't help me for the sake of the other one. By the habit I wear, you'll repent for this, *tempore et loco prelibatis*.'[172]

Then Gymnast dismounted and, climbing into the walnut tree, lifted the Monk by his gussets with one hand, and with the other freed his visor from the broken branch. And thus he let him fall to the ground, and he jumped down after. Once he'd landed, the Monk stripped off his entire harness and strewed the pieces, one after the other, all over the field; he picked up his staff and cross, and climbed back onto his horse, which Eudemon had held onto to stop him running away.

And so they merrily continued on their journey, following the path to the Willow Grove.

CHAPTER 43

How Picrochole's reconnoitring party was met by Gargantua;
and how the Monk killed Captain Chargeahead

When Picrochole heard the report of those who had escaped the rout when Tripet lost his tripes, he was seized with fierce anger, learning that those devils had attacked his men; and he held council all that night. There, Hastycalf and Swashbuckler decided that his forces were so powerful that he could defeat all the devils in hell if they showed up. Picrochole didn't altogether believe this, but he couldn't discount the possibility either.

So, in order to spy out the lie of the land, he sent out, led by Count Chargeahead, sixteen hundred knights mounted on light horses to reconnoitre, all of them well sprinkled with holy water, and each of them having as a badge a stole worn slantwise, against all hazards, so that if they encountered the devils, the virtue both of this Gregorian water and of the stoles would make them disappear and fade away.

These men galloped as far as the outskirts of La Vauguyon and La Maladerie, but they couldn't find a single person to talk to. So they came back along the upper road, and in the lodgings and pastoral hut near Le Couldray they found the five pilgrims. They tied them up and jeered at them and led them away, as if they had been spies, despite their exclamations, adjurations and requests. As they made their way down towards Seuillé, they were heard by Gargantua, who said to his men, 'Friends, we're going to meet the enemy and there's quite a number of them – ten times more than there are of us. Shall we charge them?'

'What else do you think we should do, devil take it!' said the Monk. 'Do you reckon men by number, and not by valour and boldness?' Then he shouted, 'Let's charge, you devils, let's charge!'

Hearing this, the enemy were convinced that they must really be devils, and so they galloped off in flight as fast as they could, except for Chargeahead, who couched his lance and struck the Monk a violent blow right in the middle of his stomach. But as his lance encountered the Monk's horrific habit, its iron tip was blunted, just as if you were to strike a little candle against an anvil. Then the Monk, with his staff and cross, thwacked him between the neck and the collar bone (right on the acrimion bone), so hard that he stunned him, depriving him of all sense and movement, with the result that he fell at the horse's feet. And seeing the stole he was wearing slantwise, Brother John said to Gargantua, 'This lot are mere priests – they are only just setting out on the path to monkdom. By St John, *I'm* a perfect monk; I'll pick them off like flies for you!' Then he galloped hard after them, until he caught up with the ones in the rear and beat them like rye, giving them a thorough thrashing, hitting out left and right.

Gymnast immediately asked Gargantua whether they ought to pursue them. Gargantua replied, 'Not at all. According to authentic military discipline, you must never reduce your enemy to a position of despair. If he finds himself in such straits, it increases his strength and swells his courage, which before was quite cast down and faltering. And there is no better hope of escape for men who have their backs to the wall and are completely exhausted than to have *no* hope of escape. How many victories have been wrested from the hands of the victors by the vanquished, when the former did not content themselves with being reasonable, but attempted to put everyone to death and totally destroy their enemy, without leaving a single one alive to take away the news of their defeat! You should, rather, open to your enemy every gate and way out, and rather build a silver bridge for them, so as to send them on their way.'

'Yes, but,' said Gymnast, 'they've got the Monk.'

'They've got the Monk?' said Gargantua. 'On my word of honour, they'll regret that soon enough! But so as to be prepared for all eventualities, let's not withdraw just yet; let's wait here in silence. I think I've already got a shrewd idea of what our enemies are planning. They're letting themselves be guided by chance rather than by tactics.'

And so they waited under the walnut trees, while the Monk continued his pursuit, charging against all he encountered, without having mercy on a single one. Finally he met a knight who was carrying on his crupper one of the poor pilgrims. And when the Monk wanted to attack, the pilgrim cried out, 'Ha! Sir Prior, my friend! Sir Prior, save me, I beg you!' Hearing these words, the enemy troops wheeled round, and seeing that it was only the Monk who was causing such a rumpus, they turned on him with heavy blows like those you give a wooden ass. But he didn't feel a thing, especially when they hit him on his habit, he was so thick-skinned. Then they handed him over to two archers to guard and, turning back, saw that there was no one standing against them. So they judged that Gargantua had fled with his band. And they galloped towards Walnut Grove, as hard as they could, hoping to meet them, and left the Monk there alone with two archers to guard him.

Gargantua heard the din and whinnying of the horses and said to his men, 'Friends, I can hear the tumult of our enemies, and I can already make out some of them charging en masse towards us. Let's close ranks here and hold the road, in good order. We'll then be able to meet them in a way that will do us honour and lead to their destruction.'

CHAPTER 44
How the Monk got rid of his guards;
and how Picrochole's reconnoitring party was defeated

The Monk, seeing them flee in such disorder, guessed that they were going to charge Gargantua and his men, and was deeply distressed that he couldn't help them. Then he noticed the expressions on the faces of the archers guarding him, who would gladly have gone running after the troop to get their share of the pickings, and kept gazing down into the valley towards which they were descending. He was drawing the syllogisms and saying to himself, 'These men here don't have much experience when it comes to the art of war. After all, they never asked me for my word of honour, and they haven't taken my sword off me.'

So straight away he drew the said sword and struck the archer who was holding him on the right side, cutting right through his jugular veins and the carotid arteries in his neck, together with the uvula, as far as the two adenoids; and, pulling back his sword, he slashed open the spinal marrow between the second and third vertebrae. There the archer fell, dead. And the Monk, turning his horse to the left, charged the other. When the latter saw that his companion was dead and the Monk had the advantage of him, he shouted out aloud, 'Ah! Sir Prior, I surrender! Sir Prior, my good friend! Sir Prior!' And the Monk shouted likewise, 'Sir Posterior! My friend, Sir Posterior! You're going to get a right thwack on your behind!'

'Ha!' said the archer. 'Sir Prior, old mate! Sir Prior, may God make you an abbot!'

'By the habit that I'm wearing,' said the Monk, 'I'm going to make *you* a cardinal right here! Do you ransom men in religious orders? You shall have a red hat, right now, at my hands!' And the archer kept shouting, 'Sir Prior! Sir Prior! Sir future Abbot! Sir Cardinal! Sir Everything! Hey, hey, hey, no! Sir Prior, nice little Lord Prior, I'm giving myself up to you!'

'And I'm giving you up,' said the Monk, 'to all the devils!'

Then with a single blow he cut off his head, slicing his scalp above the *os petrux*, and sweeping away the two parietal bones and the parietal suture, with the greater part of the frontal bone. In so doing, he cut through the two meninges and opened a deep wound in the two posterior ventricles of the brain; and his skull was all hanging out behind, over his shoulders, by the skin of the pericranium, in the form of a doctoral hood, black above, scarlet within. And so he fell stone dead to the ground.

After this, the Monk dug his spurs into his horse and continued along the route the enemy had taken – they had met Gargantua and his companions on the highway, and were reduced in numbers as a result of the vast slaughter that Gargantua had wrought with his huge tree, as well as Gymnast, Ponocrates, Eudemon and the rest, so that they started to withdraw in haste, alarmed and dismayed in sense and understanding, as if they had seen the very shape and figure of death before their eyes. And just as you see a donkey, when it has a Junonian gadfly at its arse,[173] or a fly that keeps stinging it, running round up and down, not knowing which way to turn, throwing off its load onto the ground, breaking its bridle and its reins, not stopping to draw breath or take a rest, and you can't tell what it is that's bugging it, since you can't see anything touching it – in the same way they fled, those men bereft of sense, without knowing the reason for their flight: they were merely being pursued by a panic terror, which had fastened onto their souls.

When the Monk saw that their one intent was to take to their heels, he got off his horse and climbed onto a great rock that was on the road, and with his great sword lashed out at those fugitives with all his might, unsparingly, not holding back in the slightest. He killed and laid low so many that his sword broke into two pieces. Then he thought to himself that that was quite enough massacring and killing, and that the rest of them should be allowed to get away so that they could take the news of their defeat with them. And so he grasped an axe from one of the men who were lying there dead and climbed back onto the rock, spending his time watching the enemy fleeing and tumbling down over the dead bodies – except that he made all of them leave their pikes, swords, lances and harquebuses, and those who were carrying the bound pilgrims he forced off their horses, and handed the latter over to the said pilgrims, keeping them with him right next to the hedgerow. And Swashbuckler, too, whom he kept as a prisoner.

CHAPTER 45
How the Monk brought the pilgrims along;
and the kind words that Grandgousier spoke to them

When this skirmish had come to an end, Gargantua withdrew with his men, except for the Monk, and at daybreak they returned to Grandgousier, who was lying in bed praying to God for their welfare and victory. And seeing them all safe and sound, he embraced them with all his heart and asked for news of the Monk. But Gargantua replied that there was no doubt but that their enemy had taken the Monk. 'That's *their* funeral!' said Grandgousier. And this had been perfectly true. Hence the proverb still in use, 'to give someone the monk'.

So he ordered a nice breakfast to be prepared for them, to refresh them. When everything was ready, they called Gargantua. But he was so full of sorrow because there was no sign of the Monk that he didn't want to eat or to drink.

Suddenly the Monk arrived, and as soon as he reached the gate of the poultry yard, he cried, 'Fresh wine, fresh wine, Gymnast, my friend!' Gymnast went out, and saw that it was Brother John leading in five pilgrims and Swashbuckler as prisoner. So Gargantua came out to meet him, and they gave him the best welcome they could, and brought him before Grandgousier, who questioned him about his whole adventure. The Monk told him everything: how he had been taken, and how he had got rid of the archers, and the butchery he had committed on the road, and how he had come to the aid of the pilgrims, and how he was bringing along Captain Swashbuckler. Then they all started to banquet merrily together.

Meanwhile, Grandgousier was questioning the pilgrims about which part of the country they came from, and where they had started out, and where they were heading for. Slowcoach answered on behalf of them all, 'My Lord, I come from Saint-Genou, in the Berry region; this chap is from Paluau; this one from Onzay; this one from Argy; and this one is from Villebrenin. We are coming from Saint-Sébastien near Nantes, and we're heading back, taking one day at a time.'

'I see,' said Gargantua, 'but what had you gone to Saint-Sébastien for?'

'We went,' said Slowcoach, 'to offer the saint our votive prayers against the plague.'

'Oh,' said Grandgousier, 'you poor guys, do you really think that the plague comes from St Sebastian?'

'Yes, we do indeed,' replied Slowcoach, 'and our preachers tell us as much.'

'Oh,' said Grandgousier, 'are false prophets spreading such illusory beliefs among you? Do they blaspheme in such a fashion against the just and saintly men of God, making them seem like devils, who do nothing but evil among human beings? Just as Homer writes that the plague was sent among the host of the Greeks by Apollo, and as the poets feign a great heap of Anti-Joves and malevolent gods? Likewise, there was one old hypocrite who used to preach at Sinays that it was St Anthony who set people's legs on fire, and St Eutrope made people dropsical, and St Gildas drove them mad, and St Genou gave them gout. But I punished him, making such an example of him – even though he called me a heretic – that ever since that time, not a single hypocrite has dared to enter my lands. And I am astonished that your king allows them to preach such scandalous nonsense throughout his kingdom. They deserve to be punished more than those who by magical art or any other stratagem have introduced the plague into the country. The plague kills the body alone; but impostors such as those poison souls.'

As he was speaking, the Monk strode in, and asked them, 'Where do you poor wretches come from then?'

'From Saint-Genou,' they said.

'And how,' asked the Monk, 'is Abbé Tranchelion, that old boozer? And what kind of life are the monks leading? Cor blimey, they're tupping your wives while you're roaming around on pilgrimage!'

'Ho ho!' said Slowcoach. 'I don't have any worries about mine. Anyone who sees her by daylight won't break his neck to go and pay her a visit at night!'

'Ooh, catty, aren't we!' said the Monk. 'She could be as ugly as Proserpina, but, by God, she'll be given a good frigging, since there are monks in the vicinity. After all, a good workman can use even the humblest materials. A pox on me if you don't find them up the duff by the time you get back home. Even the shadow of an abbey bell tower makes women fertile.'

'It's like the waters of the Nile in Egypt,' said Gargantua, 'if you believe Strabo, and Pliny, Book 7, Chapter 3, where he says that it comes from loaves, clothes and bodies.'

Then Grandgousier said, 'Off you go then, you poor chaps, in the name of God the Creator; may he be a perpetual guide to you. And from now on, don't be duped so easily by the lure of these superfluous and useless trips. Look after your families, each of you work at his vocation, educate your children and live in the way taught you by the good Apostle, St Paul. If you do this, you will have the protection of God, the angels and the saints with you, and neither plague nor any other evil will bring harm upon you!'

Then Gargantua led them into the hall for their meal. But the pilgrims did nothing but sigh, and said to Gargantua, 'Oh, how happy is the land that has such a man as its lord! We are more edified and better instructed by these words he has just spoken to us than by all the sermons that have ever been preached in our town.'

'This,' said Gargantua, 'is what Plato says, in Book 5 of the *Republic*: that republics would be happy only when kings philosophised, or philosophers were kings.'

Then he had their wallets filled with provisions, their bottles with wine, and to each of them he gave a horse to ride in comfort the rest of the way, and a few crowns to live off.

CHAPTER 46
How Grandgousier treated Swashbuckler humanely while he was a prisoner

Swashbuckler was presented to Grandgousier, and questioned by him about the enterprise and position of Picrochole, and what was his aim in raising this tumult and upheaval. The reply came that his object and design was to conquer the entire country if he could, in revenge for the insult to his cake-makers.

'He's going too far,' said Grandgousier. 'He's bitten off more than he can chew. These days, people don't go around conquering kingdoms and doing harm to our Christian neighbours and brothers. This way of mimicking the ancients – Herculeses, Alexanders, Hannibals, Scipios, Caesars and other such – is contrary to the teaching of the Gospel, by which we are each commanded to guard, protect, rule and administer our own countries and lands, and not invade those of others with hostile intent. And what the Saracens and Barbarians of bygone days called feats of arms, we now call acts of piracy and wickedness. It would have been better if he had stayed at home, governing it like a king – rather than insolently invading mine, pillaging it like an enemy. If he had governed his land he would have extended it, but by pillaging mine he will be destroyed. Be off with you, in the name of God. Follow the good; point out to your king the errors of his that you are aware of, and never give him advice for the sake of your own personal profit, for if the commonwealth is lost, so is the individual and his property. As for your ransom, I give it all to you, and desire that your weapons and your horse be returned to you. This is how things ought to be between neighbours and old friends, given that our difference of opinion isn't really a war properly speaking, just as Plato in Book 5 of the *Republic* wanted it to be called not war, but sedition, when the Greeks took up arms against each other. And if by ill fortune such war did actually come about, he commanded that it be undertaken with the greatest restraint. If you call *this* "war", it is so only superficially; it doesn't penetrate into the innermost private room of our hearts. After all, none of us is outraged in his honour, and there is no question, in the final reckoning, of having to do anything more than making up for a minor mistake committed by our men – both yours and ours, that is. Even though you were aware of the fault, you should have just let it pass, since the people involved in the quarrel were more worthy of scorn than continual resentment, especially since I had offered to satisfy their grievance. God will be a just judge of our difference, and I beg him rather to take me from this world by death, and see my property perish before my eyes, than that he should by me or mine be in the least offended.'

When he had finished speaking, he called the Monk, and in front of them all he asked him, 'Brother John, my good friend, is it you who captured Captain Swashbuckler here present?'

'Sire,' said the Monk, 'he is indeed present; he is a man of age and discretion; I prefer that you should learn it from his own confession rather than from my words.'

So Swashbuckler said, 'My Lord, it is indeed he who captured me, and I give myself up freely as his prisoner.'

'Have you set a ransom for him?' Grandgousier asked the Monk.

'No,' said the Monk. 'I'm not interested in that.'

'How much,' said Grandgousier, 'would you like for capturing him?'

'Nothing, nothing,' said the Monk, 'that's not why I did it.'

Then Grandgousier commanded that, in the presence of Swashbuckler, they should count out to the Monk sixty-two thousand saluts for capturing him. This they did; Swashbuckler, in the meantime, was given a light meal. Then Grandgousier asked him if he wanted to remain with him or if he preferred to return to his king. Swashbuckler replied that he would do as he was advised.

'Well then,' said Grandgousier, 'go back to your king, and may God be with you.' Then he gave him a fine sword from Vienne, with a golden scabbard made with fine vine-leaf ornamentation, and a golden chain weighing seven hundred and two thousand marcs, adorned with fine precious stones, to the value of one hundred and sixty thousand ducats, and ten thousand écus, as a worthy gift.

After their exchanges, Swashbuckler climbed onto his horse. Gargantua, for his security, gave him thirty men of arms and six score archers, led by Gymnast, to accompany him as far as the gates of La Roche Clermaud, if need be.

When he had gone, the Monk returned the sixty-two thousand saluts he had received, saying, 'Sire, now is not the time for you to be making such gifts. Wait until this war is over – we never know what new developments might arise. And a war waged without a good provision of money can end up panting for breath. The sinews of war is money.'

'Well,' said Grandgousier, 'when it is over I will satisfy you with a decent reward, you and all those who have served me well.'

CHAPTER 47

How Grandgousier sent for his legions; and how Swashbuckler killed Hastycalf, and was then himself killed on the orders of Picrochole

In these same days, the inhabitants of Bessé, the Marché Vieux, the Bourg Saint-Jacques, Trainneau, Parilly, Rivière, Roches Saint-Paul, Vaubreton, Pautillé, Le Bréhémont, Pont-de-Clam, Cravant, Grandmont, Les Bourdes, Chosé, Villaumaire, Huismes, Segré, Ussé, Saint-Louand, Panzoult, les Coudreaulx, Verron, Coulaines, Chosé, Varennes, Bourgueil, the Ile-Bouchard, Le Croulay, Narsay, Candé, Montsoreau and other places nearby sent ambassadors to Grandgousier, to tell him that they were apprised of the wrongs that Picrochole was committing against him. And, for the sake of their old confederation, they offered to him everything within their power, both men and money, and other munitions of war. The money from all of them together, raised through the pacts they had established, amounted to six score and fourteen million in gold. There were fifteen thousand men of arms, thirty-two thousand light horses, eighty-nine harquebusiers, one hundred and forty thousand soldiers of fortune, eleven thousand two hundred cannons, double cannons, basilisks and spiroles, and forty-seven thousand pioneers, all of them paid up and victualled for six months.

Grandgousier neither completely accepted nor completely rejected this offer. But he thanked them warmly, saying that he would settle this war by such a stratagem that there wouldn't be any need to mobilise such large numbers of decent men. He merely sent someone to bring over in good order the legions which he ordinarily kept stationed in his places at La Devinière, Chavigny, Gravot and Quinquenais, to the number of twelve hundred men of arms, thirty-six thousand infantrymen, thirteen thousand harquebusiers, two hundred pieces of heavy artillery and twenty-two thousand pioneers, all of them arranged into companies, so well provided with paymasters, quartermasters, marshals, armourers and other men necessary to the maintenance of the army, so well trained in the art of war, so well armed, so well able to recognise and follow their standards, so prompt to hear and obey their captains, so swift to run, so strong to charge, so cautious in danger, that they were more like a harmonious organ and a piece of smoothly functioning clockwork than an army or militia.

Swashbuckler arrived and presented himself to Picrochole, and recounted to him at length what he had done and seen. Finally he urged him most eloquently to reach an agreement with Grandgousier, whom he had found to be the most decent man in the world – and he added that there was neither rhyme nor reason in vexing his neighbours so, when he had only ever been well treated by them. And in regard to the main point, if they did go ahead with their plan, they would only come out of it with the greatest harm and injury. Picrochole's strength was not so great that Grandgousier would find it difficult to wipe him out.

He had not finished speaking before Hastycalf interrupted loudly, 'How unhappy is the prince who is served by men such as this – so easily corrupted, as I see Swashbuckler to be! I see that his spirit has changed so much that he would gladly have joined our enemies to fight against us and betray us, if they had been willing to keep him on. But just as valour is by all, whether friends or enemies, both praised and esteemed, so likewise is wickedness easily suspected and recognised. And even supposing that the enemy were to use this example of wickedness for their own advantage, they nonetheless always hold wicked traitors in abomination.'

At these words, Swashbuckler, filled with wrath, drew his sword and transfixed Hastycalf a little above the left nipple, whereupon he straight away died. And pulling his sword out of the body, he stoutly said, 'So perish anyone who slanders faithful servants!'

Picrochole immediately flew into a violent rage and, seeing the sword and scabbard all spattered with blood, he said, 'Was this weapon given to you so that you could treacherously slay my dearest friend Hastycalf right before my eyes?' Then he commanded his archers to shoot him to pieces. They did so there and then, so cruelly that the room ran with blood. Then he had Hastycalf's body honourably buried and Swashbuckler's thrown over the walls into the valley.

The news of these outrages was heard by the whole army; and many started to murmur against Picrochole, so much so that Grabgrape said to him, 'My Lord, I don't know how this business is going to turn out. I can see that your men are really not very confident. They feel we do not have enough provisions here, and we have already lost significant numbers of men as a result of two or three sorties. Furthermore, your enemy is being strongly reinforced by new soldiers. If once we are besieged, I can't see how we'll avoid total ruin.'

'Shit, shit!' said Picrochole. 'You're like the eels of Melun; you squeal before you're skinned. Just let them come!'

CHAPTER 48
How Gargantua attacked Picrochole in La Roche Clermaud, and defeated the army of the said Picrochole

Gargantua was given complete control of the army. His father remained in his stronghold and, encouraging them with kindly words, promised great rewards for those who performed great feats of arms. Then they reached the Ford of Vède and, on boats and lightly made bridges, they crossed over all at once. Then, considering the position of the town, which was situated in a high and advantageous place, Gargantua deliberated during the night on what was to be done.

But Gymnast said to him, 'My Lord, the nature and characteristic of the French is that they are only any good at the first onslaught. Then they are more than devils. But if they hang about, they are worse than women. I'm of the opinion that right now, once your men have drawn breath and had a bite to eat, you should order them to attack.'

This advice was welcomed. So Gargantua deployed his full army in the open field, placing his reserves on the side where the ground rose. The Monk took with him six companies of infantry and two hundred men of arms, and in great haste crossed the marshland and marched up above Le Puy and eventually reached the high road to Loudun.

Meanwhile, the attack continued. Picrochole's soldiers didn't know whether it was best to sally out and meet them, or guard the town without moving. But Picrochole made a furious sortie with a band of men of arms from his household; and there he was met and fêted with great cannon shots that hailed down onto the slopes, as the Gargantuistas withdrew downhill, so as to make more room for the artillery. Those in the town defended it as well as they could, but their shots went straight overhead without hitting anyone. Some men from Picrochole's troop, being unharmed by the artillery, charged fiercely at our men, but they gained little from doing so – they were all absorbed into our ranks and there cut down. Seeing this, they tried to retreat, but in the meantime the Monk had blocked their escape route. So they started to flee in undisciplined disorder. Some of our men wanted to give them chase, but the Monk restrained them, fearing that if they did pursue the fugitives, they would break their ranks, whereupon the defenders of the town would charge them. Then, having waited for a while and seeing nobody coming out to fight, he sent Duke Phrontiste to urge Gargantua to advance so as to reach the slope on the left and cut off Picrochole's retreat by that gateway. Gargantua hastened to do so, and sent there four legions of Sebaste's company.[174] But they couldn't gain the heights without meeting, face to face, Picrochole and the scattered troops who were accompanying him. Then they charged hard at them. However, they suffered severe injuries from those who were on the walls, firing arrows and artillery shots at them. Seeing this, Gargantua took a great force to go to their aid, and his artillery started to batter that section of the walls so intensely that all the forces defending the town were recalled to this quarter.

The Monk, seeing that the side which he was besieging was empty of soldiers and guards, bravely and boldly headed towards the stronghold and managed to gain a foothold there, together with some of his men, thinking that more alarm and panic are created by those who attack unexpectedly than by those who fight in the main body of the army. However, he held back from raising a tumult until all his men had reached the wall, apart from the two hundred men of arms whom he left behind in case of mishap. Then he uttered a horrible roar, and his men with him, and without any resistance they killed the guards who were at this gate and opened it to the men of arms, who all together ran fiercely towards the east gate, where the thick of the fighting was. And they overthrew all the enemy's forces from the rear. The besieged soldiers, seeing on every side that the Gargantuistas had captured the town, surrendered to the Monk's good mercies.

The Monk made them hand over their weapons and armour, and ordered them all to withdraw and shut themselves up in the churches, seizing all the staffs with crosses on and posting men at the doors to stop them coming out. Then, opening this same east gate, he came out to Gargantua's aid. But Picrochole thought that help was coming to him from the town, and he rashly ventured further forward than before, until Gargantua cried, 'Brother John, my friend! Brother John, you have arrived just in time! Welcome!'

Then, when Picrochole and his men knew that the situation was desperate, they fled in all directions. Gargantua pursued them to the outskirts of Vaugaudry, killing and massacring, then sounded the retreat.

CHAPTER 49
How Picrochole, in his flight, was overtaken by ill fortune; and what Gargantua did after the battle

Picrochole, in despair, fled towards the Ile-Bouchard, and when he reached the Rivière road, his horse stumbled and fell; and he was so enraged by this that in his wrath he killed the horse with his sword. Then, not finding anyone who could give him a fresh steed, he tried to take a donkey from the mill nearby. But the millers all thrashed him black and blue, and stripped him of his clothes, and gave him a filthy peasant's smock to cover himself with.

And so off he went, the poor angry man. Then, crossing the water at Port-Huault and recounting his ill fortune, he was advised by an old witch that his kingdom would be restored to him at the coming of the Cocklecranes[175].

Since then, nobody knows what's become of him. However, someone did tell me that he is at present a poor casual labourer in Lyons, and just as angry as before. And he still asks every stranger for any news of the coming of the Cocklecranes, hoping, in accordance with the old woman's prophecy, that on their arrival he will certainly be restored to his kingdom.

After their retreat, Gargantua first of all called the roll of his men and found that few of them had perished in the battle – a few foot soldiers from Captain Tolmère's band – while Ponocrates had been injured in his doublet by a harquebus shot. Then he gave them time to rest and refresh themselves, each in his company, and ordered his quartermasters to ensure this meal was paid for on their behalf, and that no outrage should be committed in the town, seeing that it was his, and after their meal they should appear in the square in front of the château, and there they would be paid for six months. This was done; then he had summoned to the same place all those who were left of Picrochole's troops, and, in the presence of all his princes and captains, he spoke to them as follows.

CHAPTER 50
Gargantua's oration to the vanquished

'Our fathers, forefathers and ancestors, for as long as memory extends, have always been of this view and this nature, that for their battles won they have preferred, as a memorial to their triumphs and victories, to erect trophies and monuments in the hearts of the vanquished by showing mercy, rather than in the lands they have conquered by building architectural showpieces. They held in greater esteem the living remembrance of human beings acquired by magnanimity than they did the mute inscriptions on arches, columns and pyramids, subject as these are to the calamities of the air, and the envy of all comers.

'You may well remember the mildness they showed the Bretons at the battle of Saint-Aubin-du-Corbier, and at the demolition of Parthenay. You have heard, and, as you heard it, admired, the good treatment they meted out to the Barbarians of Hispaniola, who had pillaged, depopulated and sacked the coastal territories of Olonne and Talmont. This whole sky echoed to the praises and congratulations that you yourselves and your fathers uttered when Arphabal, King of Canary, not content with what Fortune had already given him, invaded in fierce fury the land of Aunis, carrying out acts of piracy in all the Armorican Islands and the neighbouring regions. He was captured and vanquished in a fair naval battle by my father, may God guard and protect him.

'But what happened then? Whereas other kings and emperors, even those who call themselves Catholics, would have treated him wretchedly, imprisoned him harshly and ransomed him dearly, he treated him courteously, in all friendliness lodged him with himself in his own palace, and with incredible courtesy sent him home under safe conduct, loaded with gifts, loaded with mercies, loaded with all the offices of friendship. What was the result? Once he had returned to his lands, he assembled all the princes and states of his kingdom, described the humanity that he had experienced at our hands, and thereupon begged them to deliberate on this so that the whole world could view it as a good example. This humanity had already been, in us, a case of decent graciousness, so in them it would be one of gracious decency. There it was decreed by unanimous consent that they would offer all their lands, domains and their whole kingdom to us to do with as we saw fit. Arphabal in person immediately returned with 9,038 great merchant vessels, bringing not just the treasures of his house and royal lineage, but those of almost his entire country. Embarking to set sail by a west-north-east wind, whole crowds of people threw into them gold, silver, rings, jewels, spices, drugs and aromatic perfumes, parrots, pelicans, she-monkeys, civet cats, genets and porcupines. Not a single mother's son of any decency among them failed to throw in something special of his own. On his arrival, he wanted to kiss the feet of my father; this was deemed unworthy and was not tolerated, but he was embraced in the usual sociable way. He offered his presents; they were not accepted, as being too excessive. He yielded himself and his posterity as perpetual and voluntary slaves; this was not accepted, as it did not seem equitable. He ceded by decree of the state his lands and kingdom, offering the transaction and compact signed, sealed and ratified by all those who were required for it to be binding; this was totally refused and the contracts thrown in the fire. The end of it all was that my father started lamenting for pity and weeping copious tears, as he reflected on the frank goodwill and simplicity of the Canarians. And in exquisite words and appropriately eloquent turns of phrase, he played down the good turn he had done them, saying that all his generosity to them was worth no more than a button, and if he had indeed shown them a certain degree of decency, it was because it was simply his duty. But this made Arphabal esteem him all the more.

'What was the outcome? We could have tyrannically demanded for his ransom an extreme amount, twenty times one hundred thousand écus, and kept his older children as hostages; instead of this, they made themselves our perpetual tributaries, and obliged themselves to give us, each year, two millions in refined twenty-four-carat gold. This sum was paid to us here in the first year. The second year, of their own free will, they paid 2,300,000 écus; the third year, 2,600,000; the fourth, 3,000,000; and as they voluntarily continue to increase the payments, we shall be constrained to prevent them from bringing us any more. This is the nature of gratuity: time, which erodes and diminishes all things, augments and increases benefits, because one good turn liberally performed to a man of reason grows continually by noble thought and remembrance.

'And so, not wishing in any way to fail to live up to the hereditary generosity of my parents, I now absolve you and liberate you, and set you free and unconstrained as you were before. Moreover, as you go out through the gates, each of you will be paid for three months, so that you can retire to your homes and families. And you will be conducted in safety by six hundred men of arms and eight thousand foot soldiers, led by my squire Alexander, so that you will not be injured or insulted by the peasants. May God be with you!

'I regret with all my heart that Picrochole is not here. I would have made him realise that it was without my will, without any hope of increasing either my property or my reputation, that this war was waged. But since he has disappeared without trace, and nobody knows where or how he has vanished, I wish his kingdom to remain in the entire keeping of his son. Since he is still too young (he has not yet reached the age of five), he will be governed and educated by the elder princes and learned men of his kingdom. And, since a kingdom thus left desolate could easily be ruined if the greed and avarice of its adminstrators were not restrained, I order and command that Ponocrates be placed over all his tutors, with all requisite authority; he is to take close care of the child, until he sees that he is capable of reigning and ruling by himself.

'I am aware that a too lax and dissolute penchant for pardoning malefactors gives them an excuse for doing evil more easily forthwith, thanks to their pernicious overconfidence that they will be treated mercifully. I am aware that Moses, the mildest man on earth in his time, punished harshly the mutinous and seditious from among the people of Israel. I am aware of the example of Julius Caesar, an emperor so gentle that of him Cicero says that his fortune was most sovereign in that he could save and pardon every man, and that his virtue was likewise most sovereign in that he desired so to do; and yet even he in certain cases rigorously punished the authors of rebellion. Considering these examples, I order you to hand over to me, before you leave, first that fine fellow Marquet, who was the origin and first cause of this war, through his vain presumptuousness; secondly his friends the cake-makers, who failed to correct his headstrong behaviour straight away; and finally all the councillors, captains, officers and domestics of Picrochole, who incited him, flattered him or advised him to overstep his boundaries and come to trouble us so.'

After this oration by Gargantua, the rebels he had requested were handed over to him, with the exception of Ruffian, Shitload and Smallfry, who had fled six hours before the battle – one of them had made straight for the Col d'Agnello, without a halt, another had gone to the Val de Vire, and the other to Logroño, without looking behind them or stopping to draw breath on the way.[176] And two cake-makers were also absent, as they had perished in the battle. Gargantua did no more harm to the captives than to order them to operate the presses of his printing house, which he had just recently set up.

Then, he had those who had been slain buried with all due honour in the valley of the Walnut Grove and in the field of Bruslevielle. He had the wounded bandaged and treated in his great nosocomium[177]. Then he considered the damage done to the town and its inhabitants, and he had them reimbursed for all their losses, once they had made a declaration of what they had suffered, and sworn on oath it was accurate. And there he had a strong castle built, assigning soldiers and a watch so that in future the inhabitants would be better able to defend themselves against sudden uprisings. Before leaving, he graciously thanked all the soldiers of his legions who had assisted in this defeat, and sent them back to winter in their stations and garrisons – with the exception of some members of the Decuman Legion,[178] whom he had seen performing great deeds on the field of battle, and the captains of the companies, whom he brought back with him to Grandgousier.

When he saw them arriving, good old Grandgousier was so filled with joy that it would be impossible to describe it. So he laid on for them the most magnificent, the most copious and the most delicious feast that had been seen ever since the times of King Ahasuerus.[179] When they rose from table, he distributed to each of them all the ornaments on his sideboard, to the tune of 1,800,014 gold bezants' worth of great antique vessels, great pots, great bowls, great cups, great glasses, pitchers, candelabras, goblets, vases, jardinières for violets, comfit boxes and other such sorts of plate, all in solid gold, not to mention the precious stones, enamel, and the fine workmanship which in the reckoning of everyone exceeded in value the worth of the material they were made from. In addition, he had counted out to everyone there, from his coffers, twelve hundred thousand merry clinking crowns. And what's more, to each and every one of them he gave in perpetuity (unless they died without heirs) his châteaux and neighbouring lands, whichever were most convenient for them. To Ponocrates, he gave La Roche Clermaud; to Gymnast, Le Couldray; to Eudemon, Montpensier; to Tolmère, Le Rivau; to Ithybole, Montsoreau; to Acamas, Candé; Varennes to Chronacte; Gravot to Sebaste; Quinquenais to Alexander; Ligré to Sophrone; and so on with the other places he owned.

CHAPTER 52
How Gargantua had the Abbey of Thelema built for the Monk

That just left the Monk to be provided for. Gargantua wanted to make him Abbot of Seuillé, but he refused. He wanted to give him the Abbey of Bourgueil, or of Saint-Florent, whichever suited him best, or indeed both, if he was willing to take them. But the Monk replied in no uncertain terms that he wished to have no responsibility for, or governance of, monks. 'How,' said he, 'could I ever govern anyone else, since I cannot govern myself? If it seems to you that I have done you, and will be able in the future to do you, any agreeable service, give me permission to found an abbey in accordance with my own plans.'

Gargantua liked this request, and he offered his entire land of Thelema[180], next to the River Loire, two leagues away from the great forest of Port Huault. And the Monk asked Gargantua to establish his religious order in such a way that it would be the direct opposite of all others.

'In that case,' said Gargantua, 'there must be, to begin with, no walls ever built around it. All other abbeys are proudly walled in.'

'Yes, indeed,' said the Monk. 'And there's a very good reason for that: where there's a wall, there's a way – for gossip, envy and backbiting to flourish inside.'

In addition, seeing that, in certain monasteries in this world, if any woman enters (even decent, modest types of women), it's the monks' custom to wash the place they have passed through, it was ordered that if any monk or nun happened to come into *this* one, they would scrub and scour out every place where he or she had passed.

And because in the religious orders of this world everything is compassed, limited and regulated by hours, it was decreed that in this one there wouldn't be a single clock or sundial. But all jobs would be distributed and carried out in accordance with the occasions and opportunities that offered themselves. After all, said Gargantua, the greatest waste of time he knew of was to count the hours – what good ever comes of *that*? – and the greatest foolishness in the world lay in governing yourself by the chiming of a bell, and not by the dictates of common sense and reasonableness.

In addition, since at that time the only women who were put into convents were one-eyed, lame, humpbacked, ugly, misshapen, mad, stupid, bewitched and blemished, just as the only men put into monasteries were rheumy, low-born simpletons unwelcome in any household…

('By the way,' said the Monk, 'what good is a woman, when she's neither pretty nor good? What's she worth? As much as a piece of cloth?'

'You can make a nun of her,' said Gargantua.

'Yes, and you can make shirts out of a piece of cloth,' said the Monk.)

…anyway, for these reasons, it was ordered that only pretty women would be accepted here, well educated and of good nature, and handsome men, well educated and of good nature too.

In addition, because men never managed to get into women's convents except on the sly, clandestinely, it was decreed that women would never be allowed there unless there were men too, and men could never be there unless there were also women.

In addition, because both men and women, once they have been accepted into their order after their year's probation, are forced and constrained to remain there for ever, their whole lives long, it was laid down that both the men and the women accepted here would be able to leave whenever they wanted to, freely and entirely.

In addition, because monks and nuns ordinarily made three vows, viz., chastity, poverty and obedience, it was decreed that in this one they could be honourably married, wealthy and able to live in freedom.

As regards the legitimate age, women were taken in there from the age of ten to the age of fifteen. And men from the age of twelve to the age of eighteen.

<h2 style="text-align:center">CHAPTER 53</h2>

How the Abbey of Thelema was built and endowed

For the building and furnishing of the abbey, Gargantua had a consignment of 2,700,831 gold coins figuring a nice long-woolled Agnus Dei delivered, up front, every year, until the whole building was completed, and he assigned from the receipts of La Dive 1,669,000 sunny crowns, and the same number again of gold coins with the powdery Pleiades on them. For its foundation and upkeep he gave in perpetuity 2,369,514 rose nobles as freehold endowment, guaranteed and payable each year at the gate of the abbey.[181]

The building was hexagonal in shape, so that at each corner was built a great round tower with a diameter of sixty paces. And they were all alike in width and external appearance. The River Loire flowed to the northerly side. On its bank was set one of the towers, named Arctic. Facing the east was another called Calaer. The following one, Anatolia. The next one, Mesembrine. The next one, Hesperia, and the last, Cruaer.[182] Between each tower there was a distance of 312 paces. The whole building had six storeys, including as one of these the under-ground cellars. The second storey was vaulted in the shape of a basket handle. The rest had ceilings that were made of Flanders gypsum, in the shape of lamp bases. The roof was covered with fine slate, and, on the crest, with a topping of lead figures of little manikins and animals that went well together and were all gilded, with gutters coming out of the wall between the windows painted diagonally in gold and azure right down to the ground, where they finished in great channels that all led to the river under the lodge.

This building was a hundred times more magnificent than Bonivet, or Chambord, or Chantilly. It had 9,332 chambers, each one furnished with an inner room, study, privy and chapel, and opening out into a great hall. Between each tower, in the middle of the body of the building, there was a winding staircase built into the same structure; its steps were partly in porphyry, partly in Numidian stone, partly in serpentine marble, all of them twenty-two feet long – and three fingers thick – placed in groups of twelve between each landing. On each landing there were two fine antique arches, through which the daylight fell; and through these you came into a study with latticed windows, of the same width as the aforementioned staircase; and it reached as high as the pinnacle of the roof, and there ended in a pavilion. Through this staircase, you came out on either side into a great hall, and from the halls into the chambers.

From the Arctic Tower to the Cruaer were the beautiful great libraries for Greek, Latin, Hebrew, French, Tuscan and Spanish, arranged on different storeys by language. In the middle was a wonderful spiral staircase, which you reached from outside the building, the entry being topped by an arch six fathoms wide. It was made symmetrically, and big enough for six men of arms to ride abreast, lances couched on their thighs, right up to the top of the building.

From the Anatolia Tower to the Mesembrine, there were beautiful great galleries, all painted with ancient feats of arms, histories and representations of the earth. In the middle was a similar way up, and a gate, just as we have mentioned with regard to the side facing the river. On this gate was written in great ancient letters the following words.

CHAPTER 54
The inscription on the great gate of Thelema

Keep out, you two-faced, lying hypocrites, [183]
Old humbuggers, Vandals, Goths, Ostrogoths,
You fuddy-duddy sanctimonious shits,
Time-serving, shuffling, slippery old gits,
You persecuting pack of murderous bigots
With hatred in your hearts, who pile the faggots

Upon the pyre and watch as the flames rise…
Get lost! In here you'll not peddle your lies.

   Your wicked deceit
   Would soil our retreat
   With evil intent.
   On evil bent
   You'd soil our retreat
   With wicked deceit.

Keep out, you greedy, ignorant, bent judges
Wrapped in the mystery of your legal fogs,
Straining at gnats, you scribes and Pharisees,
M'unlearnèd friends, who pluck from parishes
Good Christian folk and kill them off like dogs.
You ought to be strung up, you filthy hogs!
There's nothing here to arouse self-righteous bile,
Or give you any excuse for a nice trial.

   Trials and debates
   Are out of place
   In this domain.
   Here joy can reign.
   Keep from this place
   Trials and debates.

Keep out, you usurers, mean-spirited bankers,
You tight-arsed, stingy, grasping, covetous lot.
Yes, raise your interest rates, you load of wankers!
And grab the loot for which your heart so hankers:
It's in our interest to see you rot!
You're never satisfied with what you've got.
So live it up in this world's fleshpot, Edom –
I doubt you'll ever come to Abraham's bosom.

Cold-hearted crew
Begone with you
Keep your pitiless hand
Far from our land.
Be off with you,
Cold-hearted crew!

Keep out, you husbands sour and warped and jealous,
Imprisoning desire in chains and locks.
You murmurous, sneeping, cowardly, seditious
Hatchers of plots and stratagems pernicious,
Like wolves ready to pounce upon our flocks,
And, even worse, you werewolves: keep your pox,
Your mangy scabs and running sores away,
And come not near our house by night nor day.

Honour's at home,
And gladly within
We all make mirth,
All in good health
Are here within
Where honour's at home.

Come in, brave knights, and welcome to you, sirs,
And doubly welcome! Bring your money too,
It's triply welcome here; wealth is a source
From which we can your comforts reinforce
And keep you with us, great and small. For though
You swarm here in your thousands, each of you
Will be my bosom pal, my dearest friend,
My close companion, now and without end.

Noble and strong,
Never doing wrong,
Averse to all evil
Courteous and civil,

Never doing wrong,
Courteous and strong.

Come in, all you who spread the Gospel word
In all its power and subtlety – you'll find
A refuge and safe haven. Undeterred
You can take shelter from the hostile brood
Who propagate error, poisoning the world.
Come in, you've found true faith; here true faith found;
And then confound, in writing and in speech,
The enemies of all who God's word preach.

The holy word
Must always be heard
On this sacred ground.
Let each be crowned
And each be adorned
With the holy word.

Come in, you ladies of high lineage,
Freely and boldly. Enter in with joy,
You flowers of beauty with your heavenly visage,
Well dressed, upright, modest, prudent and sage:
Here is the way to honour and to glory.
The noble lord, who this place did decree
And furnish, ordered thus, and gave much gold
So that you'd nothing lack here in his fold.

Gold freely given
Means he's forgiven
Who freely gave.
And so long live
All mortal men
Who gold have given.

CHAPTER 55
A description of the manor of the Thelemites

In the middle of the inner court there was a magnificent fountain in fine alabaster. Above it, the three Graces, with cornucopias. And water was gushing out from their breasts, mouths, ears, eyes and other openings of their bodies.

The inside of the lodging on this inner court was set on great pillars of chalcedony and porphyry, with fine antique arches; inside them were beautiful galleries, long and spacious, decorated with paintings and the horns of stags, unicorns, rhinoceroses and hippopotamuses, and the teeth of elephants and other things worth seeing.

The ladies' lodgings extended from the Arctic Tower to the Mesembrine gate. The men occupied the rest. In front of these ladies' lodgings, between the first two towers, there were, on the outside, to provide them with entertainment, the lists, the hippodrome, the theatre and the swimming pools, as well as the marvellous three-level baths, well provided with every kind of furnishing and a plentiful supply of myrtle water. Next to the river was the beautiful pleasure garden. In the middle of this, the fine labyrinth. Between the two other towers were the tennis courts and the court for the big ball game. On the same side as the Cruaer Tower was the orchard, full of every kind of fruit tree, all of them arranged in quincunxes. At the end was the great park, swarming with every kind of wild animal. Between the third towers were the targets for the harquebus, the bow and the crossbow. The pantries were outside the Hesperia Tower, one storey high. The stable was beyond the pantries. The falconry was this side of them, run by falconers who were experts in their art; and it was replenished each year by Candiots, Venetians and Sarmatians, with the best birds of every species – eagles, gerfalcons, goshawks, sakers, lanners, falcons, sparrowhawks, merlins and others – so well trained and tamed that, on leaving the château to go and disport in the fields, they would catch everything they encountered. The dog kennels were a little further on in the direction of the park. All the halls, chambers and studies were carpeted in various ways, depending on what season of the year it was. The whole floor was covered with green cloth. The beds were all embroidered. In each inner chamber there was a mirror of crystal, set in a fine gold frame decorated all round with pearls, and of such a size that it could really reflect the whole person. At the exit from the ladies' lodgings were the perfumers and hairdressers, through whose hands the men would pass on their way to visit the ladies. Each morning they would sprinkle the ladies' chambers with rose water, orange-flower water and myrtle water, and each lady would be provided with a precious bowl emitting the odour of every kind of aromatic drug.

CHAPTER 56
How the monks and nuns of Thelema were dressed

At the time the abbey was founded, the ladies dressed in whatever way pleased them and struck them as most appropriate. Later, they were reformed at their own free request, in the following way.

They wore scarlet or purple hose, which rose just three fingers above the knee. And this hem was nicely embroidered and indented. The garters were the same colour as their bracelets, covering the knee above and below. The shoes, pumps and slippers were made of crimson, red or purple velvet, shaped like lobster wattles. Above the smock they wore a beautiful basquine in a fine silk camblet. Over this, they wore a farthingale in taffeta – white, red, tawny, grey, etc. Above it, a frock of silver taffeta, embroidered in fine gold and interlaced with needle-work, or – if they felt like it, and depending on what the weather was like – in satin, damask or velvet, in orange, tawny, green, ashen, blue, light brown, crimson, white, in cloth of gold, cloth of silver, in purl or embroidery, depending on which feast day it was. The dresses, depending on the season, were of cloth of gold with a silver fringe, of red satin covered with gold purl, of taffeta either white, blue, black, tawny, silk serge, silk camblet, velvet, cloth of silver, silver cambrick, spun gold, velvet or satin purfled with gold in various shapes. In summer, on some days they would wear, instead of dresses, fine short surcoats with the same adornments, or else Moorish-style burnouses, in purple velvet with gold fringes over silver purl, or with golden cord garnished at the crossings with little Indian pearls. And they always had a fine panache, the same colour as the cuffs and finely adorned with gold pendants. In winter, dresses of taffeta in the same colours as above, fur trimmed with lynx, black weasel, Calabrian martens, sable and other kinds of precious fur. The rosaries, rings, chains and carcanets were of beautiful precious stones, carbuncles, rubies, Balas rubies, diamonds, sapphires, emeralds, turquoises, garnets, agates, beryls, and large and small pearls of excellent quality.

Their headgear varied with the weather. In winter, it was French style; in spring, Spanish style; in summer, Tuscan style, except for festivals and Sundays, when they wore French headgear, since this is more honourable and gives a better impression of matronly modesty.

The men were dressed in their own fashion. They wore hose of worsted or serge cloth, in white or black half-grain. Their breeches were in the same or very similar colours, embroidered and indented in accordance with their own designs. Their doublet was in cloth of gold, cloth of silver, velvet, satin, damask or taffeta, in the same colours, indented, embroidered and arranged in perfect shape. The points were of silk, in the same colours, with golden tags of fine enamel work. The coats and jerkins were of cloth of gold, cloth of silver, or velvet purfled to taste. Their robes were as precious as those of the ladies. Their silk belts were the same colours as their jerkins. Each of them wore a fine sword at his side, with a gilded handle, the sheath made of velvet the same colour as the breeches, the end made of gold and gold work. The dagger likewise. They wore hats of black velvet, decorated with many gold rings and buttons. With a white plume above, daintily divided up by golden spangles, from which dangled beautiful pendants of rubies, emeralds, etc.

But there was such sympathy between the men and women that, every day, they were dressed in the same attire. And so they would never fail in this, certain gentlemen were given the task of telling the men every morning what livery the women wanted to wear on that particular day – everything being done at the behest of the ladies.

In getting these neat, clean clothes and rich accoutrements ready, don't imagine that the men or the women wasted a single moment. The masters of their wardrobes had all the clothes ready each morning, and the chambermaids were so well trained that in an instant they were all ready and dressed from head to foot. And so they would have easier access to these accoutrements, there was, around the Wood of Thelema, a great row of houses half a league long, well lit and harmonious, where lived the goldsmiths, the lapidaries, the embroiderers, the tailors, the makers of gold thread, the velvet-makers, the tapestry-makers and upholsterers, and there they each worked at their own trade, and all they did was for the aforementioned monks and nuns. They were provided with the raw materials by the offices of Lord Nausiclete, who each year brought to them seven shiploads from the Isles of Perlas and the Cannibals, laden with gold ingots, raw silk, pearls and precious stones. If some pearls started to show their age and lose their original whiteness, the craftsmen revamped them by giving them to some handsome roosters to eat, in the same way castings are given to falcons.

CHAPTER 57
How the Thelemites' way of life was regulated

Their whole life was lived, not in accordance with laws, statutes or rules, but by their own choosing and free will. They got up when they felt like it; they drank, ate, worked and slept when they so desired. Nobody woke them up, nobody forced them either to drink, or to eat, or to do anything else at all. This is how Gargantua had laid it down. In their rule, there was only one clause: DO WHATEVER YOU WANT. This is because free, well-born, well-educated people, thoroughly at home in decent company, by nature have an instinct and goad which always impel them to carry out virtuous deeds, and hold them back from vice: this they call 'honour'. These people, when by vile subjection and constraint they are oppressed and enslaved, call on the noble feelings by which they freely tend towards virtue, and throw off and set aside this yoke of servitude. We always try to do things that have been forbidden to us and desire whatever has been denied us.

Thanks to this liberty, they fell into a laudable emulation to do all at once whatever they saw a single person was enjoying. If any man or woman said, 'Let's have a drink!' they all had a drink. If he or she said,

'Let's all play!' they all played. If he or she said, 'Let's go and have fun out in the fields,' they all went. If it was to go hawking or hunting, the ladies, mounted on fine hackneys with their proud palfrey, each of them on her daintily gloved wrist carried either a sparrowhawk, or a lanner, or a merlin. The men carried the other birds.

They were so nobly educated that there was no one among either men or women who couldn't read, write, sing, play harmonious instruments, speak five or six languages, and in these languages compose both in verse and prose. Never were seen such valiant knights, so gallant, so dextrous on foot and on horseback, more nimble, agile, and better able to handle weapons of every kind, than were these men. Never were seen such fair ladies, so dainty, less tiresome, more skilled at handiwork, with the needle, and at every decent and liberal feminine accomplishment, than the women who lived here.

For this reason, when the time had come for any man from this abbey, either at the request of his parents or for other causes, to express the desire to leave, he would take with him one of the ladies, the one who had taken him as her devoted suitor, and they got married. And just as they had lived in Thelema in devotion and friendship, all the more did they continue to do so once they were married, loving each other until the end of their days just as much as they had on their wedding day.

I mustn't forget to set down a riddle for you – it was discovered in the abbey's foundations, written on a great bronze plate. It went as follows.

CHAPTER 58
The riddle found in the foundations of the abbey of the Thelemites

Poor mortals, who for happiness all pray,
Lift up your hearts, hear what I have to say:
If we're allowed to think that stars on high,
And heavenly bodies, help us prophesy,
In our own minds, the things that are to come,
And tell the future of the years that loom,
Or if we can with aid divine foretell

The fate and destiny that awaits us all,
So that we can have knowledge firm and strong
Of what's reserved for us the years along,
I here proclaim to all who wish to hear
That in the winter of this very year,
Or even earlier, right here, we'll see
A group of men emerge who all will be
Tired of repose and glad now to be free.
They'll stir up mischief, and quite openly
Suborn all sorts of people, and arouse
Them to unleash harsh conflict and the noise
Of battle. Anyone who deigns to follow
The bad example that they set, and swallow
Their empty phrases, will find that he's soon
Opposed to friends and relatives. The son
Emboldened will not fear the deep disgrace
Of showing defiance to his father's face.
Even the great, who come of noble stock,
Will see their subjects threatening to attack.
Order and rank will then have had their day;
Honour and reverence will flee away,
For they will say that each must take his turn
To serve and then to be served in return;
And on this point there will be such dispute,
Toings and froings, tumult in the court,
That every earlier marvel will seem trite
Compared to the excitement of this fight.
For many a valorous champion will appear
Spurred on by youth's ambition and, I fear,
Will so devote himself to this great strife,
He'll leave worn out, or even lose his life.
And anyone who takes the field will find
He cannot rest until he leaves behind
Tumult of applause that to the skies
Resounds, and his skilled footwork draws all eyes.
And then, people will trust men of no faith,

More than if those men always told the truth;
For everyone of sense will find he's cowed
By the tumultuous ignorance of the crowd,
And they will choose an umpire quite inept –
Not one who's strict and fair, but lax and wet!
Wet, yes indeed, for he will sit and sweat
And never judge aright. The players, too,
Will get into a lather and a stew
While drops of perspiration from them fall
As if they danced in some wild, frenzied ball,
And they'll be parched and drenched at once, so fierce
Will be their lust to win that they no tears
Will shed over the sacrifice they make
Of herds of innocent beasts, whose guts they take
And string them out on instruments of war –
Not that they hope the gods their sins will wash
Away, but to provide a perfect forearm smash.
But meanwhile, see if you can think of all
The things that might this round machine befall,
And whether there is any hope of rest
When everyone is hell-bent on the quest
To win. What fate awaits this sphere? The best
That it can hope for is that when the dust
Of battle settles, it has not been burst
So that its maker has to take it home
And patch it up in time for the next game.
And that can take a while. The sun will set
Upon the match before you can say, 'Let…
The earth's round globe be swallowed up in night!'
Dark as a box on which the lid fits tight
The damaged sphere will be enclosed to wait
Until its maker can decide its fate.
And so it lies, of liberty bereft;
To make it whole again requires much craft.
In any case, the tremblings of this sphere
Have been as great as those which Jupiter

Caused on the earth when Etna he hurled down
On Typhon, who violence had done
Against him. The entire great globe did quake
And shudder at the awesome thunderstroke;
Nor did the mountain where the Titan lay
In bondage hurl itself into the sea
With greater fury as the monster roared
And shook beneath, when god on Titan warred.
Even a sphere restored to its first form
After such heavy knocks will seem forlorn
Again, and need to be exchanged
For one that's nice and round, as if re-made.
Eventually the time will come to call
A halt and say, 'Game, set and match!' as all
The sweat and heat of battle will suggest
That everyone should now retire to rest.
And yet, before they separate, the air
Will burn with a ferocious, blazing fire,
The open flames of a great conflagration
That ends the conflict and the inundation.
And now that they've concluded this great war,
The winners can with mirth and joy restore
Themselves, and having earned their full reward
Of heaven's manna, be, with full accord,
Enriched. The losers go away with nothing.
If you should seek a reason for all this, just think
It's what each player is predestined to.
For thus it was agreed; it shall be so.
Blessèd is he who perseveres till then –
He is to be praised and honoured by all men.

When the reading of this document had been finished, Gargantua heaved a deep sigh and said to those who were there, 'It's not just at this moment that people who have been brought back to evangelical beliefs are being persecuted. But blessed is he, whoever shall not be offended, and who shall always aim at the target, the mark, which God by his dear Son has set before us, without being distracted or led astray by his fleshly desires.

The Monk said, 'What is your understanding of the sense and significance of this riddle?'

'What?' said Gargantua. 'The discourse and maintenance of the divine truth.'

'By St Goderan,' said the Monk, 'that's not how I understand it. The style is that of Merlin the Prophet.[184] You can put as many serious allegories and interpretations on it as you want to. For my part, I think that the only meaning enclosed in it is the description of a tennis match under a veil of dark words. The suborners of men are those who set up the matches, who are usually friends! And after the two chases, the one who was in the court, serving, goes off, and the other one comes on. They believe the first one who says whether the tennis ball has gone above or below the net. The water is the sweat. The racket strings are made of the guts of sheep or goats. The round machine is the ball. After the game, they take refreshment in front of a blazing fire and change their shirts. And they are glad to enjoy a feast – those who have won being particularly happy. Cheers!'

NOTES

(NB: all translations are from the Latin, unless otherwise indicated.)

1. The last three of these are imaginary works mentioned in the first two real ones.

2. 'Brother Boobius' represents the lazy, ignorant monks whom Rabelais satirised. He is here condemned for trying (as many writers did) to read moral allegories into Ovid's *Metamorphoses*.

3. The Greek orator Demosthenes was also notorious for drinking water rather than wine. He is here the archetypal sober sourpuss.

4. These, like the vast majority of the place names in *Gargantua*, refer to real places in Rabelais's home territory near Chinon.

5. 'Drinking here'.

6. This poem is extremely obscure. There is an undercurrent of hostility to the Holy Roman Emperor, Charles V, and the Papacy (references to 'mitre' and 'tiara'); and also, in the last stanzas, a longing for peace and the purification of the Church and contemporary society.

7. 'Flutterbies': Rabelais uses the French word '*parpaillons*', i.e, '*papillons*' or 'butterflies' but also legendary savages hostile to Christianity and, by extension, Protestants ('*parpaillot*' = Calvinist, heretic).

8. This parody of the language of legal treatises seems to draw largely on Rabelais's reading of works by his lawyer friend André Tiraqueau, and in any case Rabelais himself was a trained lawyer. He here deliberately jumbles his sources.

9. It is also Macrobius who tells the story about Octavian's daughter Julia.

10. Like many of Rabelais's terms, this stream of definitions is taken from French regional dialect, in this case from Poitou.

11. 'Privation presupposes habitual possession.'

12. From Horace: 'Is there any man whom the abundance of glasses has not made eloquent?'

13. From Psalms XIX.5, 'like a bridegroom', and CXLIII.6, '[my soul thirsteth after thee], as a thirsty land', respectively.

14. 'Have due regard for the person; pour enough for two; *bus* [i.e., in French, "having been drunk"] is not in usage.'

15. Jacques Coeur was one of the wealthiest men of the French Renaissance. His house in Bourges can still be seen.

16. Conceivably, if improbably, a reference to the King Milinda who questioned Nagasena about Buddhism; otherwise, Rabelais is referring to the Melinda he places in Zanzibar (see p. 25).

17. Basque: 'Companions, let's drink!'

18. 'I thirst' (Christ on the cross: John XIX.28).

19. The Greek word '*asbestos*' means 'incombustible'.

20. Jérôme de Hangest (d. 1538) was a celebrated theologian of Le Mans.

21. Argus and Briareus were Giants: the first had a hundred eyes, all of which were put to sleep by Mercury; the second had a hundred arms.

22. La Devinière: the house in which Rabelais was born, near Chinon.

23. 'From this [the glass] into this [the mouth]': an allusion to Psalm LXXV.8.

24. 'Nature abhors a vacuum.'

25. The story of the devil and the parchment goes back to Jacobus de Voragine's *Golden Legend*.

26. These references to the strange and unnatural births of pagan myth have a subtext: are they any more or less credible than the story of the Virgin birth of Christ?

27. Scotist theologians: followers of the great scholastic theologian Duns Scotus, whose philosophy, in the over-subtle and over-academicised version Rabelais knew first hand, provides the butt of many of his jokes. The Sorbonne, another of Rabelais's *bêtes noires*, was the Faculty of Theology of the University of Paris and the arbiter, within France, of religious orthodoxy.

28. Jean Denyau: a common name in the Chinon region. It is probable that Rabelais was referring to a real person.

29. William of Occam was another scholastic theologian targeted by Rabelais. The *Exposables* (*Exponibilia*), here attributed to an apocryphal author, form a section in the *Summulae logicales* of Peter of Spain, unlikely to have been known by Occam and in any case unforthcoming on the subject of breeches.

30. Emerald seems to have been prized, in fact, sometimes for its qualities as a bromide and sometimes as an aphrodisiac.

31. Rhea entrusted the infant Jupiter to these nymphs, who offered the young god a cornucopia of flowers and fruits.

32. The Marranos of Spain were Jews who had converted to Christianity, but whose devotion to their new faith was the cause of considerable suspicion on the part of the Inquisition.

33. Humbert of Pracontal was a notorious corsair in the service of Francis I. This may be an allusion to him.

34. The myth of the androgynous origin of humanity, as told by the comic poet Aristophanes in Plato's *Symposium*, is immediately followed by the Greek of St Paul: 'Charity [...] seeketh not her own' (I Corinthians, XIII.5).

35. Nekhepso, king of Egypt (seventh century BC), was reputedly a great magician.

36. Saint-Louand was the site of a Benedictine priory. Rabelais is suggesting that it was home to devotees of the Jewish Cabbala, which was in vogue during the Renaissance.

37. Michel Chappuis was a captain of the vessel of Francis I: Rabelais, here appearing in his anagrammatical alias Alcofribas Nasier, had dealings with him.

38. Hans Carvel is a fictitious character. The Fuggers of Augsburg were one of the wealthiest banking families of the time.

39. This was a real book, by one Carroset, published at Lyons in 1528.

40. High hats had been the fashion in the reign of Louis XI (r. 1416–83).

41. Rabelais here mocks, but also plays on, the Renaissance vogue for rebuses and emblems.

42. Rabelais owned a copy of the work by the apocryphal Orus Apollo. The *Hypnerotomachia Polyphilii* (*The Sleep-Love-Combat of Polyphilius*) was a beautifully illustrated emblem-strewn fantasy by Francesco Colonna, published in 1499.

43. Admiral Philippe Chabot had as his emblem the dolphin-and-anchor symbol first used by Augustus Caesar. The speed of the dolphin, combined with the retardant quality of the anchor, produced the meaning *festina lente*, or more haste, less speed.

44. The humanist Lorenzo Valla criticised the legal writer Bartolus for what was in his view a misguided interpretation of the significance of the colour white.

45. The story was that an old woman said, as she was dying, 'the light is good'.

46. The story of Tobit, a devout Jew in exile afflicted by blindness, is one of the books of the biblical Apocrypha (though not part of the Hebrew Bible).

47. Alba Longa, the 'long white town' in Latium, founded by Ascanius, son of Aeneas, near the site of the future Rome.

48. Proclus was a Neoplatonist and pupil of Plotinus.

49. This deluge of references is almost entirely taken from the encyclopedic work by Ravisius Textor known as the *Officina*.

50. This and the expressions which follow mingle proverbs with the everyday activities of a young boy.

51. In all these places, the steep hills sometimes mean that stables are indeed cut into the rock behind and above a house.

52. Tubal and Holofernes are both biblical names: the former was a descendant of Cain and a metalworker; the latter (his name implies 'confusion', 'worldliness') was a general of Nebuchadnezzar killed by Judith. The works mentioned figured prominently in the syllabus of late medieval schools.

53. *De modis significandi*, the title of a medieval treatise on grammar. The learned commentators are apocryphal and the conclusion to which they lead the young Gargantua ('there was no certain knowledge to be gained from the *Modes of Signifying*') suitably sceptical.

54. The poetically named *Compost* may refer to a calendar.

55. All these works were mocked by the humanists. 'Seneca' is probably a pseudo-Seneca, not the first-century-AD Roman moralist. *Dormi secure* was the title of a compendium of ready-made sermons for lazy preachers.

56. Some have seen Erasmus in the otherwise obscure figure here mentioned.

57. Eudemon: from a Greek word meaning 'happy, fortunate'.

58. 'Mataiologians', a Rabelaisian nonce-word calqued on the Greek '*mataiologoi*', those people who utter 'vain jangling', according to I Timothy I.6–7.

59. Ponocrates: from Greek words meaning 'hard-working', 'strong'.

60. François de Fayolles launched an attack on the coasts of Africa, hence the comic title.

61. 'Languegoth', a word forged from 'Languedoc' and 'Goth'. The latter had connotations of Dark Age barbarity for Rabelais, and he may have been alluding to the University of Toulouse, a centre of anti-humanist reaction in the 1530s.

62. Brother Jean Thenaud published an account (*c.* 1530) of a journey across the seas to,

among other places, the Middle East.

63. There was a Babin who cobbled shoes in Chinon.

64. A *proficiat* was an offering made by a bishop to his diocese on arrival to take up a post.

65. The Latin name for Paris, Lutetia, was sometimes etymologically linked to a comment by Strabo calling it the white (in Greek, *leukos*) city.

66. The author and his book are apocryphal; the etymology is based on a similarity between the name Paris and the Greek '*parrhesia*', i.e. frankness and boldness of speech.

67. Members of the Order of St Anthony were thought able to cure pigs (and St Anthony himself is often depicted with a pig).

68. The 'oracle of Lutetia' may refer to the 'syndic' of the Sorbonne and enemy of the humanists, Noël Béda, who was exiled to a distance of twenty leagues from Paris.

69. *Baralipton* was one of the figures of the syllogism as studied in medieval logic.

70. Rabelais first wrote 'our master Janotus de Bragmardo' ('Bragmardo' implies 'sword', and thus 'penis'), making Janotus out to be a theologian. The prickly susceptibilities of the age made him replace this with the word 'sophist', which in his work is often a code word for 'theologian'.

71. A lyripipion was the hood worn by an academic theologian.

72. The dirtiness of Parisian students was legendary.

73. Philotimon's name comes from Greek words implying that he 'likes cutting things up'.

74. Janotus speaks dog Latin. '*Mna dies*' = 'g'day'; '*et vobis*' = 'and to you too'.

75. There is in fact a Londres in Cahors and a Bordeaux in Brie, but Rabelais surely wanted to make Janotus' geography seem surreal by setting London in south-west France. His language parodies late scholastic philosophy.

76. 'And a wise man will not abhor them' (cf. Ecclesiasticus XXXVIII.4).

77. To 'metagrobolise' is to sieve things, thus to consider them too curiously.

78. 'Render unto Caesar the things which be Caesar's, and unto God the things which be God's' (Luke XX.25). '*Ibi jacet lepus*' means 'there lies the hare', i.e., in scholastic jargon, 'that's the main point'.

79. Ungrammatical Latin: 'Let's have a real blow-out. I've killed a pig and I've got some lovely wine'.

80. 'For God's sake give us back our bells.'

81. Latin gibberish, with a vague recollection of the sermons of the Dominican Leonardo Matthei d'Utino.

82. 'D'you want some pardons? Well, blimey, you can have 'em, free, gratis and for nothing!'

83. 'The bells! The bells! Give 'em back! Jiminy, they're the pride and joy of our town.'

84. '… our Faculty, which is compared with the stupid mares, and is made like them, in that psalm, erm, I don't know which one [actually Psalm XLVIII.12, "Nevertheless man being in honour abideth not: he is like the beasts that perish", with a mocking side glance at the Sorbonne establishment]'. A 'good Achilles' is a clinching argument.

85. 'My argument is as follows: every bell that can be belled, belling in the belfry where belling takes place, in the bellative case makes bellable bells bell. Paris has bells. QED!'

86. A garbled reminiscence of medieval syllogistic figures.

87. 'In the name of the Father, the Son and the Holy Spirit, Amen'.

88. 'Who lives and reigns, world without end, Amen'.

89. A random scattershot of pompous Latin conjunctions basically implying 'whence and wherefore'.

90. Pontanus (the French poet Pontan, d. 1503) hated the sound of bells. The pun on 'Tapponus' is another reference to their detestable tintinnabulation.

91. 'Bye for now, and let's have a round of applause! That's all, folks!' The first tag ended the comedies of Terence, the second is a (jumbled) way of signing off a written work.

92. These anecdotes are again taken from Ravisius Textor (see note 49 above).

93. Democritus and Heraclitus, two Greek philosophers who represented laughter and tears respectively.

94. Daydreamer ('Songe-Creux') was the stage name of a famous '*farceur*'.

95. More scholastic merriment. *Suppositions*: a reference to the subtleties of medieval logic and semantics. The *Parva logicalia* were supplements to Aristotelian logic. '*Panus…*' means 'To what is the cloth related?'

96. 'Confusedly and distributively', i.e. (approximately) 'each should have his share'.

97. Not 'how' but 'to what it relates'.

98. 'To my shins'.

99. 'I, myself, will carry them, as that which is supposed bears that which is apposed' (more logical terms).

100. Patelin: hero of a medieval farce.

101. The Mathurins: a place where the Sorbonne theologians would debate.

102. 'All things that arise fall into nothing.'

103. Chilo of Sparta was one of the Seven Sages of Greece.

104. Bière: another name for the Forest of Fontainebleau.

105. Psalm CXXVII.2: 'It is vain for you to rise up early.'

106. 'Hence the couplet.'

107. This list of games (216 of them) begins with card games before moving on to common children's games of every kind.

108. 'Canonically' because the *Canon* [i.e. law] *of Medicine* was the title of a work by the Persian philosopher and physician Ibn Sina (Latinised as Avicenna, 980–1037).

109. In fact, the Greek music teacher Timotheus made pupils he had taken over from other teachers pay twice as much as entirely new pupils.

110. Basché is a village near Chinon; Anagnostes, from a Greek word meaning 'reader'.

111. The tennis (or '*jeu de paume*') court of la Bracque, in the Latin Quarter, was situated where today's Place de l'Estrapade is.

112. Tunstal, Bishop of Durham, secretary of Henry VIII and author of a book on arithmetic.

113. There was indeed a famous horse trainer based in Ferrara, which Rabelais visited in 1533–4.

114. The Latin word '*desultorius*' referred to a horse used for acrobatics.

115. Milo of Crotona, a famous athlete of ancient times.

116. All authors celebrated for their knowledge of botany.

117. Rhizotome, from Greek words meaning 'cutter of roots'.

118. Leonicus had just published a treatise on the game of knucklebones (jacks); Lascaris was a contemporary Greek scholar.

119. Rabelais was the first to use the French word '*automates*' in this sense.

120. The Picrocholine War is a homage to and parody of the wars detailed in the great epics (the *Iliad*, the *Aeneid* and their medieval and Renaissance successors) with which Rabelais was familiar. It takes place in Rabelais's own homeland: the place names and even the names of some of the participants are real. The griddle cakes that are the cause of the hostilities are known as *fouaces*, and are still a regional speciality.

121. Picrochole: from Greek words meaning 'black-biled, bitter'.

122. i.e. all those who have a voice in the monks' chapter are to go there now.

123. Litanies 'against the ambushes of the enemy'; responses 'for peace'.

124. A panic-stricken stuttering of one of the breviary responses for Sundays in October, '*Impetum inimicorum ne timueritis*', 'You shall not fear the assault of your enemies.'

125. 'Give me a drink!'

126. The friar has not been identified.

127. Rabelais was critical of the cult of the saints. The Holy Shroud of Chambéry, having survived the fire of 1532, was later moved to Turin.

128. 'I confess! Have mercy! Into thy hands!'

129. A very crooked road near Chinon.

130. A reference to the chivalric epics of the Middle Ages.

131. Hercules was said to have erected two columns at the Straits of Gibraltar, with the words '*Nec plus ultra*' ('Go no further'). The motto of the Holy Roman Emperor Charles V was '*plus oultre*', i.e. 'further', and some scholars have seen in the many variants of this phrase in *Gargantua* an expression of Rabelais's hostility to the Emperor's expansionist policies (i.e. maybe Picrochole = Charles V).

132. Barbarossa (Khayr ad-Din) was a Turkish corsair of Rabelais's age.

133. Julian the Apostate was killed on campaign against the Persians (363 AD).

134. The Easterlings are the inhabitants of the Hanseatic towns on the Baltic (the 'Sandy Sea' of a few lines down).

135. Echephron, from a Greek word meaning 'sensible'.

136. This fable, current in Rabelais's day, was later reworked by La Fontaine.

137. Sardanapalus was renowned for his feminine pastimes.

138. A medieval dialogue between Solomon and Marcon (or rather Marcoul) had brought out the high wisdom of the former and the more earthy common sense of the latter.

139. Drinkable gold.

140. From the Greek liturgy: 'God is Holy', an exclamation believed to get rid of devils.

141. From the Latin liturgy: 'From the wicked enemy [i.e. the devil], good Lord, deliver us.'

142. Aelian was a Greek Stoic who taught at Rome, and wrote on history and natural history.

143. Hippiatry is the art of treating horses.

144. The apocryphal work is a *Supplement* to the *Supplement of the Chronicles* by Philip of Bergamo.

145. The Collège de Montaigu was famous for its squalor. The young Erasmus was miserable there. Its principal was Noël Béda.

146. Saint-Innocent was the site of the big cemetery in Paris in which beggars squatted.

147. Phenicopter is the generic name for flamingo.

148. From Psalm CXXIV.2–3, '[If it had not been the Lord who was on our side], when men rose up against us: Then they had swallowed us up quick.' This application of the Psalm to an everyday (or in this case surreal) occurrence is a good example (why not?) of living exegesis.

149. Same Psalm, 3–4, 'When their wrath was kindled against us: Then the waters had overwhelmed us.'

150. Verses 4–5, 'The stream had gone over our soul: Then the proud waters had gone over our soul.'

151. Verse 6, 'Blessed be the Lord who hath not given us as a prey to their teeth. Our soul is escaped as a bird out of the snare of the fowlers.'

152. Verses 7–8, 'The snare is broken, and we are escaped. Our help [is in the name of the Lord, who made heaven and earth].'

153. 'In the statutes of my (monastic) order'.

154. 'Corpus Christi Bayard!' ('*Fête Dieu Bayard!*') was the favourite oath of the famous French knight Pierre Terrail, Lord of Bayard (d. 1524).

155. Pavia: the site of the battle (24th February 1525) at which Francis I was captured by the Spanish, an event that was felt to be deeply humiliating by the French.

156. 'Must', i.e. must of grapes, or unfermented wine.

157. From the breviary, service for lauds at the Feast of the Circumcision and the Vigils of the Epiphany: 'the root of Jesse has grown'.

158. 'The greatest clerics are not the wisest.'

159. From Virgil, *Georgics*, IV.168: '[The bees]drive away from their dwellings the hornets, that lazy tribe.'

160. 'Why? Because…'

161. 'By the shape of the nose is recognised the "to thee I have lifted up,"' with an allusion to Psalm CXXIV.1, 'Unto thee lift I up mine eyes,' and to the belief that a man endowed with a big nose is equally handsomely provided for elsewhere.

162. 'Blessed is he whose [transgression is forgiven]': the opening words of the second of the Seven Penitential Psalms (Psalm XXXII).

163. Falconry terms. Castings are pellets disgorged by hawks, and tirings are tough morsels given to them to chew on.

164. The reference to Fécamp is unclear, though the basic sense – that the offices are kept nice and short – is obvious.

165. A Latin proverb: 'A brief prayer penetrates to the skies; long drinking empties the glasses.'

166. 'O come let us drink', a play on *Venite adoremus*.

167. From the title of a section of the Decretals: *Frigid Women and Bewitched* [i.e. Impotent] *Men*. The Decretals as a collection comprise an important part of canon law.

168. Absalom, the rebellious son of King David, caught his head in the thick leaves of a tree while riding under it. While hanging there, he was slain (II Samuel, XVIII.9–15).

169. The Decretals of Gregory apparently do recommend extracting confession from those in danger of death, rather than offering practical help to them.

170. 'On holding the world and its fleeting nature in contempt.'

171. 'A monk in a cloister / Is not worth two eggs; / But when he leaves it, / He's worth a good thirty.'

172. 'At the right time and place.'

173. Jupiter had his way with Io, daughter of the King of Argos. She was changed into a cow, either by him (to disguise her) or by his wife, Juno, (to punish her); Juno then sent a gadfly to torment her.

174. 'Phrontiste' and 'Sebaste' are from Greek words meaning 'prudent' and 'respectable' respectively.

175. The Cocklecranes are mythical Rabelaisian birds.

176. They flee in three different directions: to Italy, Normandy and Spain respectively.

177. A Latin word calqued on the Greek, meaning 'hospital'.

178. The Tenth (crack) Legion in the Roman army.

179. Esther, I.1–9, describes the feasts of the Persian monarch Xerxes.

180. 'Thelema' is Greek for 'will' (as in the Lord's Prayer: '*genetheto to thelema sou*' = 'Thy will be done').

181. These coins bore the image of a sun, a Lamb of God and (a few lines further on) a rose of York. Those representing the Pleiades are of Rabelais's coinage.

182. The names of the towers are from the Greek: Arctic (= North); Calaer (= Fine air); Anatolia (= East); Mesembrine (= South); Hesperia (= West); Cruaer (= Icy air).

183. Those not welcome in Thelema are, from stanza to stanza: hypocrites; lawyers; usurers and financiers; jealous husbands and the 'poxy' servants they use to frustrate true lovers. It is notable that wealth itself is welcome (Stanza 5), presumably so long as it circulates freely.

184. Apart from Rabelais's opening two lines, and last six, the poem is by Mellin de Saint-Gelais. It adopts the language of epic (and that of the apocalyptic, Merlinesque prophecy) to describe – as Brother John points out – a tennis match, though Gargantua interprets it as a condemnation of the persecution of evangelicals by the Church.

BIOGRAPHICAL NOTE

Little is known for certain of the life of François Rabelais. He was born around 1490, most likely at his father's estate of La Devinière, near Chinon. His father, Antoine Rabelais, was probably a lawyer.

Rabelais entered the noviciate and was trained in the Franciscan monastery of Fontenay-le-Comte at Poitou, where he had received holy orders by 1521. He requested, however, and was granted, permission to leave the Franciscan order and entered the Benedictine monastery of Maillezais. He had not remained long at the latter monastery before he left, this time without permission, and began to study medicine. He became a bachelor of medicine in 1530.

Rabelais lectured on the history of medicine at Montpellier and then, in 1532, at Lyons. In the same year he published *Pantagruel*, the first of his series of giant-stories, based on local folktales. The book was extremely popular and was followed two years later by the second book, *Gargantua*, but both were banned by the Sorbonne and by the French parliament for their unorthodox treatment of religious subjects and their obscenities.

In 1536 Rabelais returned to his studies and entered the monastery of Saint-Maur-les-Fossés, receiving his doctorate the following year. Again he lectured on medicine in France and Italy, until finally, in 1546, the moderate King Francis I granted Rabelais permission to print the third book in the Pantagruel cycle, *Le Tiers Livre des faicts et dicts héroïques du bon Pantagruel*. This book, like the others, was condemned by the authorities, though it remained in print anonymously. The fourth book in the series, *Le Quart Livre de Pantagruel*, was published in 1552, and Rabelais died the following year in Paris.

Andrew Brown studied at the University of Cambridge, where he taught French for many years. He now works as a freelance teacher and translator. He is the author of *Roland Barthes: the Figures of Writing* (OUP, 1993), and his translations include *For a Night of Love* by Emile Zola, *The Jinx* by Théophile Gautier, *Colonel Chabert* by Honoré de Balzac, *Memoirs of an Egotist* by Stendhal, and *Butterball* by Guy de Maupassant, all published by Hesperus Press.

HESPERUS PRESS – 100 PAGES

Hesperus Press, as suggested by the Latin motto, is committed to bringing near what is far – far both in space and time. Works written by the greatest authors, and unjustly neglected or simply little known in the English-speaking world, are made accessible through new translations and a completely fresh editorial approach. Through these short classic works, each around 100 pages in length, the reader will be introduced to the greatest writers from all times and all cultures.

For more information on Hesperus Press, please visit our website: **www.hesperuspress.com**

ET REMOTISSIMA PROPE

SELECTED TITLES FROM HESPERUS PRESS

Author	Title	Foreword writer
Pietro Aretino	*The School of Whoredom*	Paul Bailey
Jane Austen	*Love and Friendship*	Fay Weldon
Honoré de Balzac	*Colonel Chabert*	A.N. Wilson
Charles Baudelaire	*On Wine and Hashish*	Margaret Drabble
Giovanni Boccaccio	*Life of Dante*	A.N. Wilson
Charlotte Brontë	*The Green Dwarf*	Libby Purves
Mikhail Bulgakov	*The Fatal Eggs*	Doris Lessing
Giacomo Casanova	*The Duel*	Tim Parks
Miguel de Cervantes	*The Dialogue of the Dogs*	
Anton Chekhov	*The Story of a Nobody*	Louis de Bernières
Wilkie Collins	*Who Killed Zebedee?*	Martin Jarvis
Arthur Conan Doyle	*The Tragedy of the Korosko*	Tony Robinson
William Congreve	*Incognita*	Peter Ackroyd
Joseph Conrad	*Heart of Darkness*	A.N. Wilson
Gabriele D'Annunzio	*The Book of the Virgins*	Tim Parks
Dante Alighieri	*New Life*	Louis de Bernières
Daniel Defoe	*The King of Pirates*	Peter Ackroyd
Marquis de Sade	*Incest*	Janet Street-Porter
Charles Dickens	*The Haunted House*	Peter Ackroyd
Fyodor Dostoevsky	*Poor People*	Charlotte Hobson
Joseph von Eichendorff	*Life of a Good-for-nothing*	
George Eliot	*Amos Barton*	Matthew Sweet
F. Scott Fitzgerald	*The Rich Boy*	John Updike
Gustave Flaubert	*Memoirs of a Madman*	Germaine Greer
E.M. Forster	*Arctic Summer*	Anita Desai
Ugo Foscolo	*Last Letters of Jacopo Ortis*	Valerio Massimo Manfredi
Elizabeth Gaskell	*Lois the Witch*	Jenny Uglow
Théophile Gautier	*The Jinx*	Gilbert Adair

André Gide	*Theseus*	
Nikolai Gogol	*The Squabble*	Patrick McCabe
Thomas Hardy	*Fellow-Townsmen*	Emma Tennant
Nathaniel Hawthorne	*Rappaccini's Daughter*	Simon Schama
E.T.A. Hoffmann	*Mademoiselle de Scudéri*	Gilbert Adair
Victor Hugo	*The Last Day of a Condemned Man*	Libby Purves
Joris-Karl Huysmans	*With the Flow*	Simon Callow
Henry James	*In the Cage*	Libby Purves
Franz Kafka	*Metamorphosis*	Martin Jarvis
Heinrich von Kleist	*The Marquise of O–*	Andrew Miller
D.H. Lawrence	*The Fox*	Doris Lessing
Leonardo da Vinci	*Prophecies*	Eraldo Affinati
Giacomo Leopardi	*Thoughts*	Edoardo Albinati
Nikolai Leskov	*Lady Macbeth of Mtsensk*	Gilbert Adair
Niccolò Machiavelli	*Life of Castruccio Castracani*	Richard Overy
Katherine Mansfield	*In a German Pension*	Linda Grant
Guy de Maupassant	*Butterball*	Germaine Greer
Herman Melville	*The Enchanted Isles*	Margaret Drabble
Francis Petrarch	*My Secret Book*	Germaine Greer
Luigi Pirandello	*Loveless Love*	
Edgar Allan Poe	*Eureka*	Sir Patrick Moore
Alexander Pope	*Scriblerus*	Peter Ackroyd
Alexander Pushkin	*Dubrovsky*	Patrick Neate
François Rabelais	*Pantagruel*	Paul Bailey
Friedrich von Schiller	*The Ghost-seer*	Martin Jarvis
Percy Bysshe Shelley	*Zastrozzi*	Germaine Greer
Stendhal	*Memoirs of an Egotist*	Doris Lessing
Robert Louis Stevenson	*Dr Jekyll and Mr Hyde*	Helen Dunmore
Theodor Storm	*The Lake of the Bees*	Alan Sillitoe
Italo Svevo	*A Perfect Hoax*	Tim Parks

Jonathan Swift	*Directions to Servants*	Colm Tóibín
W.M. Thackeray	*Rebecca and Rowena*	Matthew Sweet
Leo Tolstoy	*Hadji Murat*	Colm Tóibín
Ivan Turgenev	*Faust*	Simon Callow
Mark Twain	*The Diary of Adam and Eve*	John Updike
Giovanni Verga	*Life in the Country*	Paul Bailey
Jules Verne	*A Fantasy of Dr Ox*	Gilbert Adair
Edith Wharton	*The Touchstone*	Salley Vickers
Oscar Wilde	*The Portrait of Mr W.H.*	Peter Ackroyd
Virginia Woolf	*Carlyle's House and Other Sketches*	Doris Lessing
Virginia Woolf	*Monday or Tuesday*	Scarlett Thomas
Emile Zola	*For a Night of Love*	A.N. Wilson